A Little Loc

By the same author

Duty Free
Right Royal Remarks

A LITTLE LOCAL DIFFICULTY

A NOVEL OF THE SIXTIES

by
Michael Hill

*Illustrations
by
Trog*

HOVELLERS PRESS
DEAL KENT

First published in Great Britain in 2003
by Hovellers Press

© 2003 Michael Hill

All rights reserved. No part of this publication may be reproduced, stored in a retrieval system, or transmitted, in any form or by any means, electronic, mechanical, photocopying, recording or otherwise, without the prior permission of both the copyright owner and the above publisher.

The right of Michael Hill to be identified as the author of this work has been asserted by him in accordance
with the Copyright, Designs and Patents Act 1988.

ISBN 0-9546101-0-5

Printed in Great Britain by Mickle Print Ltd

Hovellers Press
85 Beach Street
Deal
Kent CT14 6JB

For Patricia

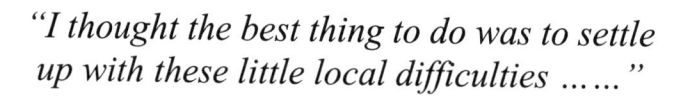

"I thought the best thing to do was to settle up with these little local difficulties ......"

Harold Macmillan (1st Earl of Stockton) as Prime Minister in 1958 speaking after the resignation of his Chancellor of the Exchequer and two Treasury ministers.

Wanda

Hilda

H-P

Benno

Quentin

Characters

Simon Lamb - a young producer at Metro TV
Pippa Crowne - a young producer at Metro TV
Tim Jago - editor of the daily programme Good Evening at Metro TV
Muriel - his secretary
Wendy - a receptionist at Metro TV
Ginger Ruddle - a film director on Good Evening
Sally - his secretary
Hopkins - an accountant at Metro TV
Hilda Fenn - Head of Programmes at Metro TV
Lord Farrier - Chairman of Metro TV
Andrew West - editor of the programme Forum at Metro TV
Wanda Haddon - a call girl, daughter of Lord Farrier
George Worthington - Home Secretary
Leo Levine - deputy editor of Good Evening
Gareth Hywel-Price "H-P" - main presenter of Good Evening
Benedict Benson "Benno" - a TV pundit
Toby Gage - a young presenter on Good Evening
Melanie - his secretary
Hammy - a commentary writer on Good Evening
Ziggy - a lift attendant
Quentin Luke - a presenter on Good Evening
Kim Adrian - a Society pimp
Kitty - a receptionist at Metro TV
Sir Roderick - Head of MI6
Carruthers – his deputy

Chapter One

The Venetian blinds were drawn against the evening sun. In the wide bed beneath crumpled sheets and a yellow coverlet a young man, Simon Lamb, lay half asleep wondering about his sexual performance. Beside him wide-awake a young woman, Pippa Crowne, was wondering if she could get a taxi in Kensington High Street.

"What's the time?"

Simon roused himself to look at the bedside clock. "Just after seven."

"Christ!"

"What's the matter?"

"Got to be somewhere," said Pippa dressing in a hurry. "Thanks a lot, Stephen…"

"*Simon.*"

"Sorry ... Simon. I mean it. Thanks. I really needed that."

"Can I ring you?"

"Do." She was gone.

Simon sat on the edge of the bed and lit a cigarette. He stared at the packet of Senior Service and dimly wondered why sailors wore beards. His head ached. He switched on the radio and heard the over-familiar sounds of Acker Bilk's 'Stranger on the Shore'. He switched it off.

At the age of twenty-two Simon had a limited experience of women. His last girl friend, a Welsh music teacher, had refused to have sex in any but the missionary position because she said it was 'undignified'. She declined fellatio because her mother had told her that it would make her grow a moustache. Also a young nurse, objecting to his somewhat unsubtle advances, suggested that he should 'get himself a German girl'. He was still puzzled by that.

It all began that lunch time when he dropped into the Queen's Elm in the Fulham Road for a quick half – "just the one!" At the bar was an acquaintance, Bill Railton, who claimed to be one of the few remaining painters left in Chelsea. By the 1960s few 'struggling artists' could afford the rents. It was thought that Bill sold phoney antiques. He once tried to sell a 'two-thousand-year-old' crucifix. More likely he lived off women. By three o'clock closing time they decided to have one-for-the-road in the Apron Strings afternoon drinking club round the corner. The Strings was in a basement, half-filled now with most of the people who had been in the Elm. It was ill-lit and stuffy - not that the drinkers appeared to notice.

After a while Simon grew bored with beer and Bill's saga of his women; he also felt the need for an Indian meal.

"I tell you what," said Bill, "There's a party this evening in Nevern Square."

"Whose party?"

"Dai something or other. Welsh bloke, works at the BBC, I think."

"Don't know him."

"You don't have to. Just bring a bottle."

"What sort?"

"Bloody old Spanish Burgundy. You know the stuff, six bob at that off licence near Finch's."

"What time?"

"Sixish. If you get there early you might get some gin."

At the door Simon turned back. "You didn't tell me the address."

The house in Nevern Square had five bells beside the front door; none of the names on the cards sounded Welsh. Noise was clearly coming from the top floor windows so Simon pushed open the door and walked up several flights of threadbare carpeted stairs until he reached the source of the noise. The room was crowded. A stocky young man confronted him. "Who are you, boy?"

"Bill Thompson invited me."

"Well, no bugger invited him," said the young man removing the bottle from Simon's grasp. " I suppose you'd better come in," and he returned to the crowd.

Simon elbowed his way to a table on which were several opened bottles of red wine, an empty bottle of Gordon's Gin, an unopened bottle of Martini and some half-used bottles of tonic. He poured some wine into a tumbler and moved into a corner by a bookcase. After a while, bored, he picked up a review copy of 'Clockwork Orange'. At that moment someone lurched into his back and a voice said, "Shit." Another voice said, "For Christ's sake, Tim."

Simon turned to find a very drunk young man wearing a scruffy bush jacket and corduroys. Looking at him wearily was a young woman. Simon studied her with interest. She had long dark hair, her eyes were pale blue; he noticed her small breasts and slim figure. She wore the standard uniform of the day, black top and plastic mini-skirt.

"Sorry," said the young man to no one in particular, spilling some wine on the carpet.

"Can't take him anywhere."

"Nor me," said Tim trying to fish a tin of Panatellas out of his pocket. Simon grabbed hold of his glass before it spilled again.

"Thanks," said the young woman, "I'm Pippa. And this ...," steadying him up, "this is Tim, in his usual state. Not that it matters."

"Nothing matters much," said Tim slurring," and few things matter at all."

"So you often say."

"I do. I do." He smiled into his glass. "Old saying." He hummed a little to himself. "You are old Father William ... I think I need to sit down."

"Oh, God," said Pippa turning to Simon, "could you help to get him out of here?"

They manoeuvred him gradually through the crowd. At the door the stocky man said, "All right, boy?" without much concern and patted Pippa on the bottom. "Mind the stairs." They minded the stairs with difficulty. In the open air Tim appeared to sober up slightly.

"He only lives round the corner in Earls Court Square," said Pippa. "Steady, for Christ's sake."

It was a spacious comfortable flat, untidy, books all over the place, a typewriter, some film cans, an expensive radiogram, bottles of wine, the bed unmade, the washing-up undone, a bachelor pad. Pippa appeared to know her way around, producing some glasses and half a pork pie. Tim slumped into an armchair, laboriously trying to light a cheroot and closed his eyes. Pippa handed Simon some pie and a glass of wine.

"Thanks. Is he often like this?"

"No, not like this, not when he's working."

"What's he do?"

"Believe it or not, he's the editor of Good Evening".

Simon was surprised and impressed. 'Good Evening' was the very popular ITV daily magazine programme. Politicians, film stars, authors, actors, dotty professors, journalists, anyone in fact in the news or analysing the news, was interviewed with an informed scepticism not previously displayed by either BBC or ITV (some reporters still greeted politicians with, 'Have you anything to tell us, Minister?'). Concise film reports ranged from the Vietnam War to meetings of the Flat Earth Society. It went out 'live' at seven o'clock and any hiccups in the studio were accepted by the nationwide audience as an amusing and integral part of the programme style. The presenters were national figures like film stars.

After a while Tim opened his eyes and peered up at Simon.

"Who are you?"

"He's the poor sod who helped you home," said Pippa.

"You did, you did." Tim reached for a glass of wine.

"Haven't you had enough."

"What is enough?"

"What indeed?" said Pippa handing him a glass. Tim took a drink still eyeing Simon.

"What do you do?" He chuckled. "And how often do you do it?"

"I had a sort of job in an Ad. Agency until last week. I was fired."

"Congratulations, old bean."

"Well…" began Simon.

"For Christ's sake," said Pippa.

"No, I didn't mean ... " Tim was struggling for words. "But sometimes when my lot complain I say, 'You might be working in advertising' and they calm down. You see?"

"I think so," said Simon.

The effort of speaking seemed to have exhausted Tim; he closed his eyes, murmuring, "Come up and see me sometime," and fell asleep snoring gently.

"Shit," said Pippa stubbing out the cheroot. "I bloody knew this would happen."

She looked at Simon. "These hot summer nights make me randy as hell. Where do you hang out?"

"Earl's Terrace".

"Let's go there." She paused. "You're not queer, are you?"

"Good lord, no."

"Well then."

In the evening light the Terrace almost recaptured some of its simple Georgian elegance, give or take a lick of paint. The blossoming lime trees partly deadened the relentless traffic noise from Kensington High Street. As they stood on the steps of number 24 an angry Irish voice up from the area said, "You're another of Tony's women then?" Peering over the railings Pippa, amused, said "Not today, I'm afraid."

"It's me, Kay," called Simon.

"Up half the night," continued the voice, "and singing and dancing on the balcony. Called me a bloody old bogtrotter they did."

"Sorry about that," said Simon opening the front door. "It's the top flat I'm afraid."

"Oh, come on," said Pippa.

The final staircase, almost vertical ("Jesus," said Pippa) led up to the flat. The living room was barely furnished with some cast-offs of the landlord, the minute kitchen was a windowless space amputated from the bathroom. The bedroom contained a large bed, a Beautility dressing-table and mirror, an ancient chest of drawers and a built-in hanging cupboard.

"Would you like a drink?" asked Simon.

"No, darling, let's get on with it. Where's the bathroom?"

Simon indicated the kitchen and went into the bedroom to tidy-up the bed. His previous girl friend had undressed with her back to him and then leapt into bed under the sheets. Pippa returned from the bathroom naked, looked around, remarked "A bit grotty," and stood admiring herself in the mirror.

"Pretty good, don't you think?"

"Yes."

She moved towards the bed.

"What are we going to use?"

"Use?" said Simon stupidly, his shirt over his head.

"French letters, for Christ's sake."

"I've got some Volpar."

"Don't trust the bloody stuff."

"Well…"

"Hold on."

She went out of the room and returned to hand Simon a pack of Durex. She grinned for the first time in a friendly way.

"You don't think I do this with everyone, do you?"

"Good lord, no."

"Well, I do. Let's get cracking."

Simon embraced her, slipping his hand between her thighs. "Screw foreplay," said Pippa, pushing him back on to the bed.

Next morning, prompted by the edginess of a faint hangover, Simon decided to take up Tim's dubious offer to visit him. He felt he had nothing to lose; perhaps he might see Pippa again.

Ignorant of North Kensington he took a taxi. His first impression was that he had been taken to the wrong address. In a street of decaying Victorian houses Metro studios resembled an abandoned factory. Discoloured concrete walls rising up five or six floors were punctuated occasionally by small metal-framed windows. At ground level there was a hangar-like door into which a lorry was disgorging a grand piano. The only clue to an identity was a small glass-fronted entrance door marked "Metrovision" in black letters. It was disillusioning to Simon brought up on those movies about Hollywood which disclosed large white studios on wide avenues bustling with activity.

"Doin' a programme are you?" asked the taxi driver.

"Just visiting."

"Better you than me. I sometimes take them home at night. Fairly smashed some of them."

Accustomed to the ghastly splendours of advertising he entered diffidently, expecting to be challenged by bemedalled commissionaires and commanded to wait indefinitely on bright modern furniture with unfriendly potted plants.

Inside was a smallish, scruffy lobby with a simple reception desk behind which a pretty blonde girl was attempting to answer three telephones and attend to two visitors. Simon hung around until the chaos subsided.

"Be an angel," said the pretty girl, "and give me a cigarette. You're not important, are you? What a morning, only my second week and I'm on my own.

Kitty's got a migraine or something. Thanks, darling." ..." Metro TV here... No, I've never heard of them. I'd try the BBC." She smiled at Simon, puffing her cigarette like a child. "I'm afraid I often say that, it gets rid of people. Did you want somebody?"

"Well, yes, he's called Tim something," adding "But I haven't an appointment."

"Darling, no one seems to have an appointment here, except possibly people who people don't actually want to see, if you get my point." The receptionist flipped through a much-thumbed phone book. "Does he do something?"

"Yes, I think he's the editor of Good Evening."

"Oh, that lot. Cheeky sods if you don't mind my saying so. I know him, Tim Jago, curly hair and spectacles. He drinks, I should know."

"Possibly. Do you think…?"

"Hold on." She dialled an extension. "Sorry." She replaced the phone. "Gardening programmes. The book must be wrong. Look, here's Fred, he's the boilerman or something. I bet he knows, been here for ages."

Fred was elderly and friendly in faded blue overalls. "Anything for you, Wendy. What's the trouble?" She explained. "Ah," said the boilerman, "he wants the cottages. You follow me, lad."

Fred led him through a strange underground passage festooned with large overhead pipes and littered with inexplicable pieces of equipment and antiquated fire buckets. At one moment a vast prehistoric boiler loomed up and Fred indicated it with affection and regret. "Been here since they made old movies in these studios. Should be in the Science Museum."

It was clearly his familiar line for newcomers. Finally they emerged into daylight and the back yard of a row of small Victorian cottages. "Here you are. Good luck, squire," and he vanished into a hut. Bewildered, Simon entered the back door of the first house. In what might have been the kitchen a thick set young man with red hair and a bushy beard was seated at a bare wooden table, feet up, telephone in hand.

"No it bloody isn't and I for one am bloody well not doing it that way, not without a sodding shot list." He had a strong north country accent. He put the phone down. "Bastards," he said, belching comfortably.

At a smaller desk, with typewriter and telephone, a girl was knitting. She regarded Simon with faint interest.

"I'm sorry. I'm looking for Tim Jago."

"Straight through, chum," said the girl. "Shit." She might well have dropped a stitch.

The next door in the dusty passageway was to the front room of the house, the sort you see from the road, always trim and empty, supposedly awaiting weddings and funerals. Someone had pasted pictures of Lenin and Rita Hayworth on the door. Simon knocked. He could hear voices within so he knocked again. From the door opposite a brisk, plain, thirtyish woman appeared.

"Go straight in whoever you are; he never answers."

She pushed open the door and they entered together. The first person he saw was Pippa sitting on an old wooden chair. She looked at him without surprise and without particular interest. Behind a large shabby wooden desk littered with papers, two telephones and a child's popgun sat Tim. Apart from a television set and a monitor, two or three more wooden chairs, a bookcase half full and an old Victorian fireplace, the room was ill-furnished. On the wall was a tattered leave roster, hand-drawn and much corrected and last year's calendar with the name of a taxi firm, showing a view of "Lovely Thailand".

"Come in," said Pippa.

Tim, mixing Alka-Seltzer in a glass, studied Simon.

"Do you know this chap?"

"I do, and so do you."

"I do?" Tim gave Simon a friendly albeit puzzled look. "Are you the time and motion man?"

"He helped to get you home, for Christ's sake.

"He's Stephen."

"Simon," said Simon.

"Ah."

"You also," said Pippa, "asked him to come and see you."

"Ah."

"So?" said Pippa.

Simon felt it was time he joined in this cryptic dialogue. "Actually, I was wondering if there were any jobs going."

Tim fiddled with his popgun. "This is my secretary, Muriel. Have we any jobs?"

"Not that I've heard of," said Muriel without looking up from her typewriter.

Tim thought for a moment. "What about the Home Secretary profile?"

"New to me."

"It's something of Hilda's."

"Nobody tells me anything."

"Well if we do it, that is if Hilda even remembers she suggested it, we'll need a researcher."

"Hopkins said no more contract staff," said Muriel.

"Not to me."

"There's a memo."

"Lost in the post," said Tim loading his popgun. Then, to Simon, "Know anything about the Home Sec.?"

"He seems… " began Simon cautiously.

"He not only seems," said Tim, "he is. The other week *Private Eye* named him the most boring politician of the year - or was it the century?"

"Oh, dear."

"Don't worry, by the time we've finished with him he'll make the front cover of *Time*, one way or another."

"Meeting," said Muriel, "You're late already."

"O.K., Stephen…"

"Simon," said Pippa.

"Yes, Simon. Take care of him, will you, darling."

"I'll try," said Pippa.

"See you later in the Club."

The Conference Room at Metro was large, windowless and unventilated. It had once been a storage space for camera equipment when the building had been a ramshackle film studio, responsible in its day for many travesties of English history. A long table of imitation oak dominated the room; on it were two carafes of grey water and several discoloured glasses. Half dozen or so editors and senior producers were already seated, smoking, chatting, their notes and clipboards in front of them. They were all under thirty, casually dressed in tieless shirts and jeans. One man, somewhat older, alone wore a dark suit with two pens in the top pocket. He clutched a neat folder; no one chatted to him.

Hilda Fenn swept into the room and the chatting ceased. "Be quiet," she barked at the ensuing silence. The legendary Head of Programmes at Metro was a stocky, dynamic woman in her sixties whose moods could change in moments from domineering anger to equally disconcerting charm. Addressed by everyone except her current favourites as Mrs Fenn little was known of the late Mr Fenn who was thought to have slipped away during the previous war. Her career as journalist and broadcaster stretched back into the mythical days of BBC radio. Some old hands wishing to establish their own credentials even suggested that she had been an unlikely girl friend of the painfully puritanical John Reith. Now in her decline, usually attended by a gin and tonic, she was the unpredictable driving force and scourge of Metro.

Hilda

Producers either crumpled or fled in terror. The chairman, Lord Farrier, alone commanded her respect. Hilda glanced eagle-eyed round the table.

"Where is Tim?"

"Traffic probably," said Andrew West loyally; he was the editor of 'Forum', the current affairs heavy weekly programme. It was an ill-timed remark. Hilda glared.

"As for you, last night's Forum was a disgrace."

"I thought the Foreign Secretary interview went rather well."

"You know I'm not talking about him, an admirable man, an Etonian, a gentleman, rare enough in politics nowadays. No, it was that dreadful discussion on legalising homosexuality."

"I thought…"

"Be quiet. You know perfectly well I will not have any homosexuality before nine o'clock."

Andrew was just about to reply when a voice said, "Nor after nine o'clock, I trust."

Tim had strolled into the room smoking a Panatella.

"Why are you late?" snapped Hilda.

"If I may say so I think you may be a trifle early," said Tim taking the only vacant seat. It was well known that he was one of Hilda's few favourites, a licensed court jester.

The weekly programme review, known as the "Chimp's Tea Party", was a highly capricious occasion depending entirely on Hilda's mood. One memorable day she threw a copy of the minutes at the editor of the gardening programme. All this when she was completely sober.

Today she ended her review of Metro's output with some sharp criticism of the BBC for their new series, 'Z Cars', which she stated would undermine respect for the police. She had been an admirer of 'Dixon of Dock Green' and his "Evening All" concern for the general public.

From time to time on matters of finance she consulted Hopkins, the accountant in the suit. He was notorious among producers for his meanness with expenses. It was thought that he disliked all programmes; his favourite comment about costs was "We're not the BBC, you know."

He passed a sheet of paper up to Hilda.

"I see from these figures that 'Good Evening' is overspent again."

"Not overspent, Hilda," said Tim, "under-budgeted."

She was about to reply when the clock in the dilapidated church opposite the studios could faintly be heard striking twelve. Bar opening time. Hilda picked up her papers and swept from the room saying, "Time to get on with your work."

Midday in Chester Square. Lord Farrier, small, dapper 54-year-old millionaire chairman of Metro, was leaving his home when he met his daughter arriving. Alice Haddon was twenty-five, a tall long-legged blonde saved from conventional English-rose beauty by full sensual lips.

"Alice, darling."

"Wanda, please, daddy."
"Sorry, I forgot. How are you?"
"Great."
"What are you doing these days?"
"Still modelling."

Lord Farrier grinned.

"Your mother isn't happy about it."
"Not respectable?"
"No."
"Not the thing?"
"No."
"No jokes about the sunny side of Jermyn Street?" said Wanda.
"Definitely not."
"What would she like me to do. Join the dolly-birds at the BBC?"
"I expect so."
"Do you want me to?" said Wanda.
"Darling, you know I don't mind what you do."
"Great."
"Take care. I must be going."
"Where are you lunching?" asked Wanda.
"White's, I expect."

Outside was an Aston Martin. Lord Farrier gave the chauffeur an address in South Kensington. Wanda strolled into the drawing room. Lady Farrier, sixty, elegant, vague, with a gentle stammer that men in their time had found beguiling, was reading the *Daily Mail*.

"Hallo, darling, I didn't expect you. Mr Dempster says that you were seen somewhere with an Arab. Is that quite the thing?"

"Mummy, darling. I wish Mr Dempster would bugger off. He was a Saudi, Daddy knows him. In fact I think you had him to dinner once."

"You know," said Lady Farrier, "I read in one of those awful Sunday papers that people like that come to London to meet prostitutes. Can that be true?"

"Call girls, mummy. It's a bit different."

"I haven't heard that expression. What do they call?"

"Darling, you sometimes forget that our family more or less started that way. Charles Two and all that…"

"I think," said Lady Farrier firmly, "that royal affairs were quite different in those days."

"What beats me," said Wanda examining the invitation cards on the chimneypiece, "is that people should be surprised when any of the royals behave badly nowadays. They've been doing it for a thousand years and I don't see why they should stop now."

"*Really,* darling."

"Anyone phoned?"

"I think there was a message from your friend Pippa. Now, there's a respectable girl."

"She'd like to hear you say that."

The Metro club was a large, sparsely furnished room with a bar along one wall. The worn carpet was stained with drink and cigarette ash. In one corner was a fruit machine that had never been known to return a jackpot. Tim joined Pippa and

Simon at the bar. "You two getting to know each other?"

The club was already filling up. One group including Fred was the electricians, carpenters and cleaners who actually kept the building going from day to day. The film editors formed their own group. Scattered about drinking beer mostly and eating salads were the production staff. Standing apart with her entourage was Hilda.

"I suppose you'd better meet the old dragon," said Tim to Simon. They moved across. "Ah, Tim, I was just saying to Barry here that producers must not be chary of consulting me at any time about programmes. Take last night's Great War episode." Metro was engaged in an interminable history of the First World War. "Gallipoli. He got the details about the hospital ship all wrong. I was there, you know..."

"You were there?" said Barry nervously.

For a brief splendid moment Tim envisaged General Liman von Sanders announcing, 'Gott in Himmel, Hilda has landed, bring up the reserves.'

"No, you silly man, of course I wasn't *there*. I was a nurse in Alexandria." She turned to Simon, "And how are all those idlers in the New York office?"

"Actually, Hilda…" began Tim.

"Yes, thank you, Barry, I will have one more. What are you trying to say, Tim? Do speak up."

"We've just had a call from the Private Office. The Home Secretary has agreed to do an interview."

"The Home Secretary?"

"Yes, Hilda. You remember your idea the other night to do a series of profiles of the Cabinet."

"Of course, of course. An estimable man. Quick on the uptake. I told him recently at a dinner, one can't help being a Harrovian. Fault of one's parents after all. He agreed. No scandal there, unlike some I will not name. Sober fellow, also unlike some. Thank you, a little more tonic." She turned to her acolytes.

"Terrible thing to see talented people destroyed by drink. My father, you know, was in the Treasury, knew Asquith. Brilliant man, sadly took to the bottle."

"Wasn't he replaced by Lloyd George?" said a visiting producer hoping to appear informed about politics.

Hilda exploded. "How dare you mention that vile man's name. I remember once as a child he patted me on the head at a Trooping the Colour. I felt there was something evil about him even then. A disgrace to politics and to the nation, especially to Wales. Such a decent, sober, God-fearing people .."

"Dylan Thomas," someone murmured, fortunately unheard. She turned back to Tim. "What was I saying?"

"The Home Secretary."

"Ah, yes, good choice to begin with. After all a useful ally when the next round of franchises comes up. Not of course that you should be influenced by that when making the programme."

"Quite."

"Nor the fact that he is a good friend of the chairman."

"Quite."

"Should make exciting television. Highlights of his career, interviews with his friends and then ten minutes of so with him. No silly jokes like cartoons or anything."

"Quite."

Hilda spied another victim and Tim and Simon returned to the bar. "What was all that about the New York office?"

"Hilda gets a trifle confused," said Tim. "She recently mistook duke Ellington when we had him on the programme for Louis Armstrong who we had on last year. She asked him about his trumpet."

"How did he take it?"

"Charming guy, he was amused. Let's have some lunch."

Chapter Two

After lunch they returned to Tim's office. "Hang around and see what's going on," he said to Simon. Gone wss the inertia of the morning. The evening's programme took shape: items were discussed, intros written, timings checked, running orders revised and coffee in plastic cups drunk. Muriel typed continuously.

Pippa entered, clipboard in hand, murmuring "Common Market?"

"Christ!" said Tim, "Not again."

"Afraid so," said Pippa. "Big Tory vote in the House against the terms for joining."

"Who can we get?"

"Shadow Foreign Sec?" said Pippa.

"Give it a try," said Tim without much enthusiasm.

A sallow-faced young man came in. He wore a red shirt and yellow tie; thick spectacles gave him an intense look. "Hello, darling." He patted Pippa; she ignored him. "This," said Tim to Simon, "is Leo Levine, the deputy editor. He's very clever, aren't you?"

"Yes."

"What are you up to?"

"Forward planning."

"Well, in that case, you'll have to forward plan Hilda's latest brainwave."

"Christ, no. What?"

"Cabinet profiles."

"Just your cup," said Pippa. "Rub shoulders with the nobs. Social climber's dream."

"Thanks, darling. Doesn't sound too bad. Who do we start with?"

The telephone rang, as on cue, and a familiar voice barked, "Tim, I've just had a good idea."

"Yes, Hilda."

Tim held the phone away from his ear.

"Don't interrupt. We should do a series of profiles of the Cabinet, starting with the Home Secretary."

"Good idea, Hilda."

"Don't argue. Just get on with it." She rang off.

"Oh, God," said Leo, "not old George Worthington."

"Afraid so."

"Get the worst out of the way, I suppose. Who's going to present?"

"Don't know yet."

"What about production staff?"

"I'll let you know."

"Some bloody series," said Leo. "However I reckon it could work if I do it my way."

"What's that?"

"Without you and Hilda interfering all the time."

"Suits me," said Tim.

"Good." He smirked at Pippa. "Bye, darling," and left the office.

Tim looked at Simon. "He's not too bad really."

"That's what you think," said Pippa.

The red-bearded man who Simon had seen earlier barged into the office. He stroked Pippa's back and she didn't seem to mind.

"Is your bloody film ready yet?" said Tim.

"Is it fuck."

"Why not?"

"M and E track trouble."

"Excuses," said Tim. "Simon, this is Ginger Ruddle, one of our talented film directors."

"Bollocks," said Ginger amiably. "How do?"

"What do you want?"

"Well…" began Ginger.

"No, we don't want to hear all that," said Tim. "What else?"

"I'd like to do a film about Dylan Thomas."

Tim groaned. "How do you see it getting past Hilda?"

"Late one evening, perhaps."

"Better you than me."

"No sweat," said Ginger, patting Pippa as he left.

Tim relaxed with his feet on the desk.

"It's all a bit of an act, Ginger. Went to Sedbergh, got a first at Leeds. Rather laid-back really."

"You could say that," said Pippa.

At 3.30 on the dot the door opened and Gareth Hywell-Price, the main presenter of the programme strode in. "Strode" was apt because he retained a military bearing from the war in which he had served with considerable gallantry and a gusto which he now displayed relentlessly on television. His craggy face, staring eyes and emphatic hand gestures were as familiar to millions of viewers as any film star. A well-cut tweed suit, gleaming brogues and a regimental tie completed an image of respectability becoming rare in television. Under his arm were the *Daily Telegraph* and the *Financial Times.* He greeted Pippa, "Hallo, my dear." Tim introduced Simon.

Gareth fixed him with his celebrated stare. "You're joining a fine programme. Our aim of course is excellence, not a word heard about enough in modern life these days, let alone television. We may not always achieve it but, by heaven, we try, don't we, Tim? Three things, my boy, to bear in mind if you want to succeed here or anywhere else for that matter: tell the truth, tell it lucidly and tell it briefly..."

Simon noticed that Tim had closed his eyes and Pippa had picked up a magazine. But the noble cascade of words that passes for wisdom among the Welsh was cut short by the telephone and Muriel saying, "Tim, its Hilda." As before, he held the phone some way from his ear.

"The Home Secretary, Tim. You haven't forgotten already, have you?"

"No, Hilda."

"I've decided that Toby can present it. Who have you got to produce it?"

"I thought…"

"No, certainly not Ruddle. Possibly Leo. Any more questions?"

"Well, I…" but Hilda had rung off.

Gareth who had been listening said, "Capital idea. George Worthington is the best Home Secretary since Chuter Ede. See him quite often at the Reform. I think that he represents…"

"Tell me," said Tim, once more checking the Rotarian eloquence, "about your author this evening."

"Ah, the great Haxhi Koleka. You've read his Albanian trilogy?"

"Can't say I have."

"Seminal work. Should have got the Nobel last year but you know what the Swedes are like. Well, I must get cracking." He gave Simon his dazzling smile and strode out of the office, followed by Pippa. "I wonder," mused Tim, "whether the chap can speak English," and he replaced the cork in his popgun.

Some while later Pippa returned. "The Opposition won't put up anyone."

"No interview, no item," said Tim, "have to be stage army," turning to Simon, "We have two or three trusties we can call on at the last moment to fill the prog."

"Who?" said Pippa.

"Old Benno, I suppose. There's a piece in *The Express* today. He's apparently joined forces with Mrs Whitehouse about too much sex on television."

"And too much television for that matter," said Pippa. "He's been on the box a lot lately saying so."

"That'll have to do," said Tim. "Book Benno. Toby can do him, he's done it before."

Simon knew about Benedict Benson. Everyone who watched television or read newspapers did. He was that recent phenomenon thrown up by television, the pundit. Gilbert Harding had nearly become one but drunkenness and early death gave him only passing fame. The requirements were the facility to hold forth lucidly, provocatively and often humorously on any subject under the sun (including possibly the sun if Patrick Moore wasn't available).

In television, as Simon was soon to realise, performance was ninety percent of the battle. No good having the world's greatest scientists, surgeons, explorers, painters or inventors if they couldn't explain in simple terms what they had done. Better get your professional commentators who couldn't work a Bunsen Burner or treat a chilblain to unravel the miracles of the laboratory or the operating theatre. Pundits took the role of the commentator a stage further with a touch of controversy, a flavour of metaphysics, a pinch of cracker-barrel philosophy. Name it and a taxi would soon have your pundit bouncing along to the nearest studio.

Old Benno had all the right credentials for punditry: Cambridge, broadsheet journalism, M.I.6 during the war and the editorship of a somewhat humorous magazine. After a rackety private life of boozing and womanising he had, at 60, declared for celibacy, teetotalism and God. It was a three-pronged fork which he wielded profitably on a medium he roundly denigrated; a splendid act, delighting the public and pleasing TV producers.

Toby Gage wandered in. Although in his late twenties he looked about seventeen with a world-weary boyishness more depraved cherub than choirboy. Make-up girls had the unusual task of making him appear older. He had arrived in television after a successful stint in radio.

"Pippa tells me that I'm doing Benno."

"Yes.

"The mixture as before," said Toby.

"Quite. But before you relax there's a real chore. Hilda wants you to do a profile of the Home Sec."

"Jesus," said Toby, "has he got a profile?"

"Up to you to give him one."

Toby considered the idea.

"Might mean lunching."

"Might well."

"Reminds me, darling," turning to Muriel, "has Hopkins passed my exes."

"He has not."

"Why not?"

"Two lunches on the same day, for heaven's sake. Who do you think you are, Jekyll and Hyde?"

Toby laughed a trifle anxiously. "Don't joke, darling. Little Melanie must have muddled the bills."

"Little Melanie," said Muriel, "is new here and not yet used to your fiddles."

"Mistake. Who's producing?"

"Probably Leo. Simon here is your researcher," said Tim.

"Hi," said Toby affably. "Can I have this?" picking up a review copy of a large book on country houses.

"As long as you don't flog it before the publication date. Now go and show Simon how to get press cuttings and such."

"Worthington, crikey," murmured Toby drifting out of the office.

The object of Metro's political interest was, as it happened, lunching that day at the Oxford and Cambridge Club in Pall Mall with an old school friend. The Rt. Hon. George Fisher Worthington, O.B.E., M.P., Secretary of State for the Home Department, preferred to spend his lunchtimes with people unconnected with politics, preferably friends who had shared his "old days" either at school or university. At the age of 52 he looked back with nostalgia to the simple values of his youth. Most of their conversation as they ate the oxtail soup, lamb chops and treacle tart was anecdotal, tales of steady promotion in House and School, the award of "colours", scholastic prizes, the Debating Society. Some boys had smoked, drunk, had sexual encounters in and out of school ("You can have one new boy for a bar of fruit and nut.") Not George.

Around them in that sombre dining-room a variety of civil servants, dons and country members chatted over half of lager or a shared bottle of claret. An occasional glance at the thickset figure of the Home Secretary reassured them that law and order at least was a brake on the unwelcome onrush of the new decade.

In his own constituency in Somerset problems were mainly agricultural. In the Commons he had, quite rightly in his opinion, rejected the Wolfenden recommendations on homosexuality and reluctantly agreed to licence betting shops. He felt at home, as it were, at the Home Office and was pleased when the press referred to him, albeit patronisingly, as a 'safe pair of hands'. His old school friend suggested a glass of port.

"I think not, Henry. By the by, do you ever watch television?"

"Not much. The Test Match, of course. Why?"

"I was wondering if you've seen a programme called Good Evening."

"Heard of it certainly. Quite popular, according to my son."

"Apparently they want to do something they call a profile of me. What do you think?"

"A sort of drawing, you mean?"

"No, no, Henry, wake up. A sort of biography about my politics of course and Cambridge and the war and so on."

"I can't remember what you did in the war."

"Cairo mostly. Staff of D.Q.M.G., interesting time."

"And Cambridge?"

"Well, not a great deal, I suppose. Secretary of the College Essay Society. I worked pretty hard, you know."

"You got in the House in '47?"

"'48. Winston gave me my first leg-up in '52 to Muck and Bricks, PUS job."

Henry ordered a port.

"Doesn't your Cabinet have a hand in television?"

"Now you mention it, we do."

"Shares are doing pretty well, the commercial lot. My broker mentioned it," said Henry.

"Quite true. I said to Archie Farrier only the other day if I were a backbencher I'd have a few of his stock. Come to think of it, I believe my office said that it's Metro who want to do this profile thing."

"I should have a word with him, George. Can't be too careful. Someone told me that one of those interviewing chaps actually suggested to a cabinet minister that he was not answering the question."

"Damned nerve. The PM knows how to deal with that sort of thing. Apparently he recently drew attention to the bias in television and the interviewing chap, cheeky fellow, asked him in what direction."

"What did he reply?" asked Henry.

"In all directions."

Simon had followed Toby up some uncarpeted stairs into a small dusty room, once a bedroom. A young, dainty, girl sitting at a desk was reading a paperback which she put away hurriedly. "Pretty grotty," said Toby indicating peeling wallpaper and a rusty fireplace. "This is Melanie - I'm afraid you'll have to do the exes again."

"Sorry, did I make a mistake?"

Toby hesitated, aware of Simon.

"Not really. It's that mean bugger Hopkins."

After glancing at his mail Toby said, "Angel, get the News Inf. cuttings on Old Benno, will you? Only the recent stuff."

"Old Benno?"

"Benedict Benson. And while you're at it, get Simon some cuttings on the Home Secretary and background stuff on the Home Office generally. Might as well make a start."

Melanie began telephoning and Toby relaxed in his chair. "How did you get this job?"

"Tim was drunk at a party."

"Very likely. Any telly experience?"

"No, I'm afraid not," said Simon.

"Don't worry about that. We nearly got landed with a researcher recently who didn't even know the name of the Prime Minister let alone the Home Sec. She was a temporary barmaid at some club and Leo promised her a job if she'd go to bed."

"Was *he* drunk?"

"Not particularly. It's his old-fashioned approach. He's prick-happy, can't be helped."

"I met him briefly," said Simon.

"He's O.K. An amiable sort of show-off. Bit too bloody ambitious for my money. He wants Tim's job of course but Tim's not half as casual as he appears, besides which he's a very good editor. Leo's a good producer, he'll do anything to get what he wants to make a programme, which is not a bad thing unless you're in his way. I reckon," said Toby, unwinding a paperclip, "that we'll do a good job on the Home Sec, that is so long as Hilda leaves us alone. Have you met her?"

"In the club. She thought I was someone from the New York office."

"Very likely. It's the drink."

"Does everyone around here drink?" asked Simon.

"Mostly. It's the hospitality cupboards, they're open all the time." Toby picked up another paper clip. "Not my vice. I'm only really interested in money and fame." He looked wistful for a moment and began opening his mail.

A few minutes later Leo came in, leered at Melanie, ignored Simon and said to Toby, "Benno is on. His new line, moderately new anyway, is that television is actually doing harm by putting people off legitimate sex, he means sex in marriage. Husbands and wives apparently see the voluptuous creatures screwing away on the box and then look rather pityingly at their own partners. He doesn't want a nine o'clock watershed thing, he wants to stop it all."

"Bit extreme?"

"Well, you know Old Benno, if he wasn't extreme he wouldn't be on the box, would he?"

"So I take the free-for-all line as usual. Play it by ear."

"Or by finger," said Leo, glancing at Melanie.

"Not funny," said Toby.

"*Doigt de seigneur*, then, as Old Benno himself said once."

"Get out."

"By the way," said Leo lingering in the doorway, "about the Home Sec., do you want me to go and see him?"

"No, Leo, I don't want you to see anyone just yet. Simon here is the researcher."

"Do you know anything about him?" asked Leo.

"Only what I've read," said Simon.

"Well, that's not a lot of help. What's the budget, Toby?"

"For Christ's sake, push off."

"Let's have a planning lunch," said Leo.

"Anything," said Toby, "so long as you leave."

"O.K., Wheeler's on Friday. I'll get my girl to book a table. I'm off to the cutting room, if you want me," and with a final leer at Melanie he left.

"Back to the prog and Old Benno," said Toby fiddling with paperclips.

"What else is there in it this evening?" asked Simon.

"At least there aren't any animals."

"Animals?" said Simon, puzzled.

"This programme for some unknown reason has a weakness for them. There was a kangaroo once that we had to manhandle behind the lift gates when it got stroppy. Then there was the chap and his wife who brought in some snakes. Frightful scene."

"Tricky things, snakes."

"Oh, they were all right. It was the couple, they had a really blistering row in hospitality."

"But what on earth were they doing on the programme?"

"You may well ask. There's a key thing, as you will discover, called "pegs". If someone can provide a peg to hang an item on anything goes. Anniversaries are the best bet. Find a peg for some damned animal and you'll be popular round here."

After a while Toby went off to the dubbing theatre and Simon returned to Tim's office where he was listening to a shambling young man holding a can of film. "It's just a man wrestling with a bear, Tim."

"I know."

"Why?"

"I don't bloody know. Isn't there any dope?"

"No."

"Well, you're the commentary writer," said Tim.

"Why are we using it?"

"Because there's a hole in the bloody programme."

"Where did it come from?"

"What's it say on the can?" Tim asked.

"Man wrestling bear."

"Hammy, for Christ's sake get on with it. Toby's got to dub the sodding thing."

"Can I borrow your popgun?"

"No."

"Can I have the day off tomorrow?"

"No."

"O.K.," said Hammy, unconcerned, wandering out of the office.

"Dreamy bugger," said Tim, "but a bloody good commentary writer. Now what?"

Muriel was on the phone: she looked despairingly at Tim. He's arrived already."

"Can't be helped," said Tim, turning to Simon. It's Old Benno. Snag is, he comes up by hired car from East Grinstead, driven by a retired policeman who either loses his way and gets here thirty seconds before we go on air or sets off in good time to avoid getting lost and arrives an hour early. Be a good chap, will you, and go down and look after him." When Simon seemed alarmed Tim added, "Don't worry, he'll do all the talking, just keep him happy, and don't let him wander to other programmes, he likes seeing old chums."

Simon went through the back room where Ginger was now sitting with his feet on his desk reading *Private Eye*. He looked up amiably. "Are you really going to work for this bloody programme?"

"I think so."

"God help you."

"Why?"

"Why? Because it's stuffed with trendy buggers from Oxford and Cambridge who don't know their pink arses from their purple elbows."

"Balls," said the pretty young secretary who had discarded her knitting and was now typing large white cards on what appeared to be a jumbo-sized typewriter. "There you are," said Ginger. "Sally's one of them too. You wouldn't think, looking at those sexy eyes, that she got a tripod…"

"Tripos, for Christ's sake."

Ginger winked crudely. "…at bloody Cambridge, all those punts and…"

"Shut up," said Sally firmly, "I've got about ten minutes to do these bloody cards."

These were the days before autocue and the presenters had to read their intros from large white cue cards, typed out on a "jumbo" with big letters, to be placed precariously beneath the lens of the studio cameras. With long intros on several cards the floor manager had to crouch beside the camera and remove each card like the person who turns the pages for a pianist.

Somehow Simon found his way back along the underground passages to the reception desk. Old Benno was chatting merrily to Wendy; they seemed on pretty intimate terms. "...position all the way, my dear, don't you believe a word of it . . ."

"Mr Benson?"

He turned sprightly blue eyes on Simon, questioning, friendly.

"I'm from Good Evening. Tim asked me to..." He hesitated to say "look after you."

"How well I know the way to hospitality," obliged Benno, "the path of good intentions that leads to Hades. Lead on." He patted Wendy's arm. "Take my advice, my dear, you're far too intelligent to loiter in this bordello." Wendy giggled with pleasure, upsetting the pile of mail on her desk. On the way to the hospitality room Benno was waylaid by two producers from other programmes delighted to stop and gossip.

Finally in the pokey little room that had over the years welcomed everyone from prime ministers to pin-ball champions Simon opened the drinks cupboard, a well-worn item of cheap furniture (which bore the marks of many a forced entry) and asked Benno what he would like.

"A mere tonic with ice and lemon, dear boy," he said wistfully. "As you may know I have foresworn the demon alcohol. A matter of age rather than asceticism, I assure you. Drink gave me, if not my friends, great pleasure in its day. Drunkenness is one of the most pleasurable and possibly forgivable sins. The only price you pay, and at my age, a trifle exorbitant, is the hangover. Don't let me stop you, the way they drink around here is positively Lucullan. All taxpayers money - better spent, after all, on booze than bureaucrats."

Simon poured the drinks, taking a very small whisky for himself.

"You are new to the infernal grove?" said Benno taking the least uncomfortable of the worn-out chairs.

"Yes, I sort of started today."

"Escape, dear boy, while the going's good. It's the devil's work, I know, I've been enslaved for years. I have the mark of Cain upon my forehead, the stigmata of television branded by that all-seeing eye of the camera that really sees only what you want it to see..." He rambled on genially as though rehearsing a familiar speech for a Foyle's lunch or a popular chat show.

"Only one thing worse, dear boy," Benno was now saying.

"Worse than what?" asked Simon.

"Telly, this ghastly box," said Benno indicating the battered old set in the corner, standing dark and silent. "You could, you know, be working in advertising."

"I was, I'm afraid."

"Out of the frying pan into the empty grate," said Benno cheerfully. "Ah, here comes Toby."

Almost immediately the two were deep in gossip. Simon thought he had better return to the offices. A slight scene was occurring at reception as he passed. A small, bald, elderly man was waving his hands desperately at a more than usually flustered Wendy.

"No, no, is not drama, is not Nazi story, is books."

"Well, Mr..." Wendy looked beseechingly in Simon's direction.

"Is books," said the visitor again.

"Angel," said Wendy to Simon as yet another desk telephone rang, "be a help, will you."

Amid the ringing telephones and the increasingly irate man she said, "I thought he must be someone for the drama serial in Studio 2, you know the thing about all those people resisting the Nazis in France or somewhere, dropping by parachute and torturing and all. I thought he was probably a Nazi." Simon suddenly realised who he might be. "Am not a Nazi," shouted the famous communist novelist. Simon said timidly, "he's Mr ... er..."

"I am always saying what I are," he said furiously.

"Quite so. He's for Good Evening," Simon said to Wendy. "I'll take him to the programme."

"Not the Nazi." Mr Koleka was doubtful but calmer.

"No, not the Nazi."

"You are an angel," said Wendy. "Have you got such a thing as a cigarette?"

Simon escorted the famous novelist to hospitality. "This," said Simon desperately, "is…"

"Am not a Nazi."

"Indeed not," said Toby. "Do have a drink," and to Simon, "Better fetch H-P."

Back in the lobby Simon bumped into Sally, Ginger's secretary. "Be a duck and take these intro cards up to the studio, will you? I'm up to my eyes."

"Where?"

"Fourth floor. Take the lift."

"They're all mad," said Wendy.

Simon pressed the lift button and with much groaning and clanking the ancient lift appeared disclosing an almost equally ancient operator. Ziggy, part Polish, part Cockney, wore a tattered Ruritanian uniform and cap. He saluted. "Good afternoon, sir. May I be of service?"

"Four, please." Gates clanged shut and the groaning and clanking restarted; the lift moved incredibly slowly. Ziggy fished in his pockets bringing out a wristwatch. "Genuine rolled gold, self-winding, works under water, how about a fiver?"

"Not really, thank you," said Simon.

Undaunted Ziggy fished again. "Packet of three. Two packets for two bob, can't say fairer." The lift shuddered to a halt within several inches of the fourth floor and Simon stumbled out with Ziggy's valedictory, "Gossamer, laddie, only the best."

By six-thirty the three hospitality rooms were crowded with presenters, producers and their guests. The rest of the programme staff was busy depleting the drinks cabinet. Simon joined the group around Pippa and Ginger. He was still surprised and hurt that she had made little effort to be friendly. Already he was aware that the Good Evening team was a close-knit group who viewed all other Metro programmes with condescension if not contempt and all strangers with suspicion. His feelings were those of the new boy's first day at school and he wondered if he would ever be accepted into their world.

Soon afterwards H-P, Toby, their two guests, and Tim and Muriel departed for the studio and everyone else settled down, drink in hand, in front of the monitors.

"No sign of Hilda," said Ginger. Someone said, "She's giving stick to 'Money Matters' down the corridor."

The last of the ads. ran its soapy course and someone turned up the volume as the company logo appeared followed by a shot of an empty studio and the jaunty programme signature tune. H-P walked briskly into shot: "Good evening. We have something of a mixed bag for you including an exclusive interview with one of the world's most talented if unhonoured authors, a would-be Nobel laureate. Then today's big question: how far can television censor itself? That master of controversy Benedict Benson joins the debate. And in the true eccentric tradition of Good Evening we sent Duncan

MacTaggart up to Yorkshire to investigate the inebriated village, a strange tale of cakes and ale. But first Toby Gage…" There followed a familiar but entertaining skirmish between Benno, the old campaigner posing as a Puritan and Toby, the clever young man posing as a libertarian.

H-P smiled tolerantly and adjusted his expression to indicate serious culture. A resume of the works of Haxhi Koleka was followed by a long first question. Then just enough time for the author to begin, "I think ..." before H-P was off on his second long question. It was a technique known in the trade as "asking the answers", and was mostly used in emergencies when the interviewee was either paralysed with nerves or drink. H-P liked the sound of his own voice.

After four minutes Tim in the gallery said, "Wind." In the studio the floor manager crouching beside a camera began circling his hand towards H-P. No reaction. "Fast wind." No reaction. "Cut-throat, for fuck's sake," said Tim. Mercifully and almost magically the great studio professional halted the interview on the dot of five minutes.

Cut to Toby looking deadpan. "Some people take their recreation by hang-gliding, pot-holing or snake-charming. One man has an even more unusual hobby..." As the bear-wrestler came up on the screen the drinkers down in hospitality fell about with laughter, ever increasing as Hammy's commentary plus some tum-te-tum music endeavoured to sustain the nonsense.

H-P shrugged faintly to disown the previous item before introducing a wonderfully bizarre film story about a Yorkshire village which had decided to bake the biggest pie in the world. "And that's all for this evening, Good Evening." Fade to black.

"Jesus bloody Christ," said Toby as he and H-P walked towards the lift. "Never again will I read a half-witted intro into a load of crap."

"A scandal," said H-P, "allowing only five minutes for one of Europe's most distinguished authors. Gave him no time to develop his theme. I can't imagine what Hilda will say." Ziggy had the lift gates open. "Well done, gentlemen. Now I have here some razor blades".

Later in hospitality (sometimes aptly referred to as 'Hostility') Benno was holding court with Toby, Leo and Sally - he liked women near him. In another room the staff were demolishing the drinks cabinet. In the third H-P was bidding farewell to a disillusioned novelist. "My apologies again, my dear fellow. They are barbarians not allowing you more time. Afraid I must leave you, I've got to speak at the Royal Television Society dinner. Bit of a chore really. Peter here will get you a taxi." He beamed at the production assistant and strode out.

"It won't take long," said Peter, adding anxiously as he saw the novelist begin to pace the room, "Please take a seat and relax."

At that moment the door flew open and Hilda entered. Peter knew his priorities. "Gin and tonic, Mrs Fenn?"

"Please.

She rounded on the novelist. "You may have got the Nobel prize for something or other but let me tell you it was certainly not for plain speaking."

"I…"

"Couldn't understand a word you were saying. I grant you H-P didn't help, always talks too much, it's the Welsh in him." She took a large gulp of gin.

"I…"

"No good re-capping now, all over and done with, but a word of advice, if ever you appear on this programme again, which is probably unlikely, no offence of course, we don't often discuss foreign novels, I would advise you to brush up on your subject."

She turned to Peter. "Now, where's old Benno?"

"In there, I think," said Peter faintly, indicating the next room.

Hilda left.

Haxhi Koleka did not just sit down, he collapsed into an armchair. Mistaken for a Nazi on arrival, unable to talk during the interview and now horribly insulted by an unknown woman. He recalled favourably his years in the Italian prison camp during the war.

Benno was indulging in his favourite topic, the sex lives of his contemporaries. Occasionally his hand brushed Sally's thigh. He was describing in some detail the latest affair of a Cabinet minister when Hilda sailed into the room. Catching only the last few words she boomed, "Quite right, Benno. Scandals like that need denouncing. If politicians can't set us an example, who can? Thank goodness for our Royal Family. I saw you trounce this young whipper-snapper," she beamed fondly at Toby, presently a court favourite. "Of course I doubt if he believes a word of it, all this so-called new morality, do you?"

"Yes," said Toby.

"Nonsense. Swinging London indeed. I haven't seen any swings, have you, Benno?"

"No," said Benno, "can't say I have."

"I should hope not. And that pill you were talking about. If it's what I suspect it is," she glared at Ginger, "I'm not an ignorant old fogey, you know. If as I suspect it's some ridiculous aphrodisiac or other the Home Secretary will soon have it banned. Now there's an exemplary politician for you. Isn't that so, Benno?"

"I'm afraid so, Hilda."

"What do you mean? Yes, thank you," she handed her glass to Toby. "You can't…"

"No, Hilda, I was about to say that I was afraid no one seems to appreciate his hidden qualities."

"Well, you'll be glad to know that *we* do. Young Toby is going to do a profile of him. Should be an example to us all. It's time I was off. I've got to speak at the Royal Television Society dinner. I'll tell them a thing or two. Where's H-P? He's giving me a lift. I'm speaking before him, thank goodness. How those Welsh do go on." She left like a Wagnerian heroine.

"Dear boy," said Benno collecting his coat, "what a terrible chore."

"I know. I know," said Toby. "Can't you help us at all?"

"Television," replied Benno, "is at its best when things are at their worst and vice-versa. Your assignment with old George comes strictly under the latter heading. Reliable, honest politicians are not only rare, they make for very boring television."

"How can we ginger the thing up?" asked Leo.

Benno paused in the doorway.

"I tell you what. Go and see Kim Adrian," and he was gone.

"We'll ask Quentin tomorrow," said Tim. "Meanwhile let's not waste valuable drinking time. Leo, fetch the bottles."

"Give you a lift," said Toby some time later to Simon, "provided you don't live in Highgate or somewhere."

"Thanks. I'll just collect my coat from the office."

As he passed through the lobby Wendy, working hard with her lipstick, remarked, "Thanks, Simon darling, for helping out with the foreign gentleman."

"He was very upset, you know, by your calling him a Nazi."

"I'm sorry, angel, but you must admit he sounded like one. I watch that programme they do in the drama studio, it's called Moonstrike and it's very exciting. The British agents have to avoid capture by the Nazis…"

"Yes, I know," said Simon patiently, "but don't you realise that the Nazis are played by British actors."

"No, darling," said Wendy completing her make-up, "I didn't know and what's more I think it's rather un-British of them."

Simon returned to the cottage and as he opened the back door to Ginger's office he saw in the half darkness that Ginger was lying back in his chair. Pippa's head was in his lap, moving leisurely, expertly, up and down.

Simon muttered "Sorry," but it was doubtful if either noticed him.

"Didn't you find it," asked Toby.

"Well, actually I..." Simon was still flustered.

"Don't tell me," said Toby switching on the engine, "they're like bloody chimps."

Chapter Three

Next morning Simon turned up at the studios at nine o'clock, office hours at the Ad. agency. Kitty, a tiny redhead, was on duty at reception.

"What do you want?"

"I think I'm working on Good Evening.

"Not now you aren't.

"What do you mean?"

"Well, duckie, they don't come in before ten, do they?"

"I didn't know."

"Go to the canteen, if I were you, you look half starved. Bring me a cheese roll, there's a sport."

Several men in overalls, including Fred, the boilerman, were sitting around eating large plates of bacon, sausage, beans, eggs and fried bread.

"What'll you like dearie?" Asked the large Jamaican woman behind the counter.

"A coffee, please."

"Help yourself, dearie."

Fred looked up as Simon passed his table.

"Did you find them?"

"Yes, thanks."

"They're all a bit potty if you ask me."

"Really?"

"Yes, it's working in television."

"How are you?" asked Simon politely.

"No coke."

Simon looked bewildered.

"Delivery, lad. No coke for the boiler."

"Does it matter too much in the summer?" Simon said for something to say.

"I don't think you know nothing about boilers, does he?" turning to his fellow eaters. They looked up at Simon from their plates and clearly considered the question too obvious to answer. "Do you want that extra bit of fried bread, Fred?" asked one.

Few things are less inspiring than an empty canteen except, possibly, a full one. After a while Simon wandered over to the office. He was surprised to hear a voice in one of the back rooms and opened the door. An elegant, young man in a pale grey lightweight suit was on the telephone.

"Yes, darling, that's all very well but if Keith doesn't want Ian to do it there's no point in putting it on in the first place. Am I right, darling, or am I not?"

He looked up from the phone and waved Simon to a chair. The conversation continued for several minutes. He tapped a pencil on the desk, smiled absently at Simon once and looked at his watch, clearly grew impatient or bored with the caller. Finally he rang off.

"Why do people not accept the inevitable? Because I suppose nothing is inevitable. Makes me sound like an old Chinese philosopher or a cracker motto. Actually, I am Quentin Luke. I work here."

Quentin

Simon knew who he was. Apart from Good Evening you couldn't switch on a chat show or glance at a gossip column without catching a glimpse of him. Charity concerts and celebrity lunches welcomed him; occasionally Shaftesbury Avenue put up his name, albeit in smaller lights. He reached into the pocket of his elegant suit and Simon almost expected him to bring out a long cigarette holder. He produced a red-backed address book and flipped through it.

"You may wonder," he said, continuing his search, "what brings me to this squalid office at the crack of dawn. Two things, I imagine. I only sleep three or four hours. Very wasteful time in bed is unless of course," he looked up, "one is not alone. Also it's amazing the amount of work one can get done before the phones start ringing and before the chatterers and cheerleaders arrive here with their busy and boring plans for the day. "

Simon murmured something about the previous evening.

"Ah yes. I didn't see the programme, there was conveniently a first night of Keith's latest play, but I hear that H-P managed to stagger us all with a stunning display of culture. What do you think of our wonderful programme?"

Simon was about to answer when Quentin continued: "As you know we've been going several years, won prizes and become something of an institution. The advantages of this are that we can get away with anything, practical jokes, animals in the studio - we had a pig for some unknown reason recently - songs and revue sketches as well ,of course, as dreary old political interviews and mad professors. We take the politicos a trifle seriously if not the dotty dons."

He stopped, ruminating, oblivious of Simon.

"Thing is, we do all these things on different occasions. Why, I often wonder in the small hours, whenever they are, why don't we, or rather I, dream up a programme which combines all these things.

Simon nodded, not wishing to break the spell.

"Just imagine," Quentin continued, beginning to weave the ideas with a light sweep of his hand. "A big studio, big enough for dancers as well as singers, revue sketches, but about what's actually happening in the news not that red-nosed Light Entertainment stuff and..." he paused, hand still, "some mickey-taking for the old politicos. Should cause a rumpus, and a rumpus is what we all need in these times, surely?"

"Yes."

"No animals, I fancy. Not just to begin with."

"No

"Hilda won't like it nor will the sixth floor, they'll say it's rocking the boat." He was weaving again. "The press might give it a fair wind - old nautical saying I picked up somewhere - if it's successful of course. Probably call it satire. Just really topical humour, that's all, just topical humour." He sat silent, absorbed in his thoughts. Then suddenly, "Good God, dear boy, it's nine-thirty and nothing done." He picked up the phone and Simon took the hint to leave.

Toby bustled in soon after ten complaining about parking. Melanie went to get coffee. "Come to the morning meeting, if you want," said Toby. "All meetings are of course a waste of time, but some people in this building have made them into a philosophical concept: I meet therefore I exist. After that we'd better give a thought to this bloody documentary."

The meeting in Tim's office was a reflection of his own laid-back attitude; people drifted in and out. Simon found Leo, Ginger and Pippa discussing last night's programme.

"Can't someone stop H-P doing these arty-farty bloody items, asked Ginger, belching slightly.

"You try it," said Leo. "Anyway, when's that film of yours going to be ready. I…"

"Yes, yes. I told you yesterday, I've got a rough-cut now."

"What's it about?" said Pippa, nodding good morning vaguely to Simon.

"It's about the Beatles."

"Who?"

"The Liverpool Sound, for Christ's sake, you must have heard of them."

"Are they as big as the Tornadoes?" asked Pippa.

"They will be."

"So you say."

"Old Benno was in good form," said Pippa.

"What never fails to surprise me," said Tim producing an ivory backscratcher from a drawer, "is that the world in general looks upon Benno as a rebel, a scourge of society, almost a revolutionary when in fact he is one of the most reactionary people I know. He's against sex, especially homosexuality, pop music, modern art, new movies, heart transplants, marijuana, TV of course. You name it, he's against it."

"Whatever you say I'm against it," chanted Leo.

"Horse feathers," said Ginger.

"Has he really given up sex?" asked Pippa.

"I'm told," said Tim scratching his back, "that over at the BBC he manages to drop his script on the floor of the dressing-room and when the young, leggy girls bend down to pick it up he goes for the quick grope."

"Good for him," said Pippa. "By the way, Leo tells me that I'm on his sodding Home Sec. thing."

"I'm afraid so, darling, I can't spare anyone else."

"I thought you'd enjoy it," said Leo, patting her knee.

"That's as far as you'll ever get," said Ginger. "Stick to your barmaids."

"Go to hell."

"Please," said Tim, "don't make it more difficult. What do you think, Simon?"

"I just wondered what Old Benno meant last night when he said, 'Ask Kim Adrian'."

"Good question. Is Quentin around?"

"I saw him." Muriel was already on the phone.

A few minutes later Quentin sauntered into the office.

"You look rather svelte," said Tim.

"Svelte, yes, I like that. Is this one your grisly meetings?"

"Tell us, who is Kim Adrian?" said Tim.

Quentin perched on the edge of Tim's desk and picked up a magazine.

"You really don't know?"

"Would we have asked, dear boy?"

"And this is a topical programme. Kim is society's favourite pimp, gossip, bon viveur, wheeler-dealer and an excellent bridge player. Is that enough?"

"More than," said Tim.

"You want me to interview him?"

"Do you know him?"

"Of course I do," said Quentin, offended. "But why this interest? Is the chairman in a spot of bother?"

"What about the chairman?" asked Leo.

"Nothing. Something I vaguely heard," said Quentin looking at his watch.

Tim explained.

"George Worthington?" said Quentin. "My dear, hardly Kim's cup of tea. But of course one never knows, does one? Look at old thingummy, no one expected him to be caught in a public loo. I tell you what, I'll be going to one of Kim's parties quite soon.

"What about me?" said Leo.

"What about you?"

"Can't I go to a party?"

"To work, comrades," said Tim, "we have a programme to produce." He turned to Simon. "What ideas have you got?" Simon consulted some rough notes.

"The economy?"

"What about the economy?"

"Piece in *The Times* about the latest figures released by the Treasury - forecast expenditure."

"Such as?"

"Six billion seven hundred and ninety-seven thousand pounds."

"Do you know what that is?"

"The cost of running the country, I suppose," said Simon.

"No. It's the most boring piece of news since, well, since the last Treasury forecast. Do you really think our viewers want to hear about 'servicing the national debt,' 'short-term interest rates' and 'GDP'?"

"No."

"Of course not. What else?"

"Art sales."

"Such as?" said Tim.

"Somerset Maugham has sold a Gauguin for £13,000."

"So?"

"Well, he bought it for 200 francs in the South Seas."

"Not a bad profit. Can we get him?"

"I doubt it," said Simon, "He's in the South of France"

"So, what else?"

"Two Renoirs went for £48,000 each and a Rembrandt fetched the world's top price at £190,000."

"So?" said Tim.

"What do you mean?"

"Look, dear boy," said Tim patiently, "we're not a bloody news programme. We're only interested in facts if we can make them illustrate a point - the price of fakes, laundering Mafia money, tax dodging ... you see?""

"Yes."

"Anything else?" asked Tim.

"Not really," said Simon shuffling his notes half-heartedly, adding, "Someone is going to retrace the journeys of Lawrence of Arabia."

"What with?"

"How do you mean? A camel, I suppose."

"Good," said Tim. "Get one."

"What?"

"Get a camel. Ages since we had an animal on the prog. Toby can write a witty intro about Lawrence. Isn't there an epic with Peter O'Toole coming out any minute from Hollywood? Try and get a clip or something."

"What…" began Simon appalled.

The telephone rang. Muriel said, "H-P on three."

"Get cracking," said Tim, "Yes, H-P."

Simon returned to Toby's office in a daze.

"What's the matter?" asked Toby.

Simon explained.

"Silly sod. Didn't I warn you?" said Toby.

"What are we to do?" said Simon, at a loss.

"Well," said Toby, long used to the eccentricities of Good Evening, "your job is to get the camel. I will ring a few contacts about film clips." To Melanie, "Get me cuttings on Lawrence." He paused, then, "T.E., darling, not D.H. Last time we asked for cuttings on James Baldwin they sent us stuff on old Stanley."

"How do I...?" began Simon.

"Chipperfield's, dear lad," said Toby, "they're always useful."

So Simon rang the circus people out at Whipsnade. "Good Evening, is it?" said a man at the zoo, unsurprised at the request. "We always like to help. Would it be a Bactrian or an Arabian? Ah, yes, Colonel Lawrence. What time would you like delivery? Certainly with a keeper. Of course he speaks English."

Simon rang Metro 'bookings'. A bright lady also seemed unsurprised. "What size would it be?"

"I really don't know. Why?"

"We pay by size and time used."

"I'll have to find out," said Simon.

"Is the camel to perform?"

"What do you mean?"

"Well," said the bookings clerk, without any trace of humour, "if the animal lifts its legs intentionally during its appearance that is performance and Equity have a different scale of fees."

"How can we tell," said Simon mustering self-control, "if it lifts its legs intentionally or accidentally?"

"What's in the script?"

"I don't think there is a script."

"In that case I don't think that it should have an ordinary drama contract. More like one as an 'extra'."

"Whatever you say."

"By the way, we keep saying 'it'. Is it male or female?"

"I really don't know. Does it matter?"

"I suppose not - unless there is another camel in the studio. We once had a lot of trouble with an Arabian Nights drama. The producer insisted on live animals. The insurance company wouldn't pay for the damage to the set."

By tea-time Simon felt that the situation was under control. Toby had organised a suitable film clip and the house foreman had been alerted to provide extra stagehands, one with a bucket of sand and a shovel.

The telephone rang. Melanie said, "Bookings again."

"Yes." said Simon.

"Has the camel got a name?"

"I don't know. Why?"

"It's standard practice with animals to issue a personal contract in case of legal trouble."

"O.K. I'll find out."

By this time word of the item had got round the programme, arousing general interest and some humour.

"Is that where humping comes from?" said Ginger.

"Terrible halitosis, I'm told," said Leo.

"Disgraceful item," said H-P. "I suppose none of you have actually read *Seven Pillars*."

At six o'clock Simon opened the hospitality cupboard and poured himself a large whisky. Ten minutes later the phone rang. "It's Wendy here,

Simon." She giggled. "Are you expecting a camel?"

"Yes."

"Well, it's arrived. The keeper wants to know what to do with it."

"Tell him to hold on."

"You are funny. It's in a van."

"I should hope so."

Simon conducted the van to the entrance used for scenery. The camel was large, smelly and well-behaved. The keeper, not at all exotic, was a plump middle-aged cockney in a pork pie hat; he held the camel by a long halter.

"What does it weigh?" asked Simon.

"About a ton, I should think."

"No, I must know more precisely."

"Why?"

"Because the scene dock lift can't take anything over a ton."

"Well then," said the keeper firmly, "Just under a ton." The camel fitted into the lift; it seemed used to confined spaces. The floor manager already alerted said resignedly, "Park it over there out of the way. I hope it doesn't fart."

At six-thirty Toby, relaxed as usual, came up to the studio for a rehearsal. He was to do a 'walk-down' past several 'Blow-ups', hugely enlarged photographs of Lawrence and the Arabs, whilst he gave the intro.

"O.K. cue Toby," said the floor manager. The boom microphone swung overhead. Next moment there was an unexpected crunching noise over the foldback speaker. The camel, quiescent at the side of the studio, had suddenly seen a pineapple-shaped object on a stick wave into its line of sight and quite naturally extended its huge tongue to investigate. The keeper caught off guard, quickly restored order. "Sorry, mate."

"Very droll," said Toby, unflappable as ever.

"I refuse," said H-P, "to have anything whatsoever to do with this appalling item."

"You don't have to," said Tim. "Just hand over to Toby."

All went well. Toby did his witty intro, the camera panned all over the camel which behaved impeccably, not lifting its feet, nor needing the sand bucket. Down in hospitality the drinkers shrieked with laughter. Fortunately, and Tim had checked this in advance, Hilda was out of town and with any luck out of view.

A few days later two lunches took place.

One was at Wheeler's Alcove in Kensington High Street where Toby, Leo and Simon had their first planning meeting. The tables in the long narrow room were occupied by quiet, sober-suited residents of Kensington, a few handsome women in light summer dresses, an occasional diplomat from one of the nearby embassies. Toby spread his napkin and without looking at the menu ordered half-a-dozen oysters and lobster Thermidor; from the wine waiter a Campari soda and a bottle of white burgundy.

"Always start," he said briskly, "as you mean to go on." Leo and Simon studied the menu. "I suppose," said Toby ordering another bottle some ten minutes later, "that we have to talk shop sometime."

Leo looked at Simon, adding, "A brief, a very brief biog. do you think?"

New to planning lunches, Simon asked if he might refer to some notes; it seemed a social gaffe. He lowered his voice: "George Fisher Worthington, age fifty-two, educated Harrow and Selwyn, Cambridge, First in History, merchant banking, army, major on staff, O.B.E., entered Parliament 1948…"

"…and then up the greasy pole to the Home Office," said Toby.

"Married with two children at university," added Simon. There was a long silence broken by discreet laughter from a nearby table.

Toby roused himself by pouring some wine. "One thing about this restaurant, the waiters don't come creeping around to pour your wine, very irritating habit. Where does he stand in the party?"

"Typical Tory," said Leo.

"I think," said Toby, "we've had enough shop for one day, don't you?" And much later, "That trolley looks rather inviting."

The bill came to £21.

"Have we a project number?" asked Toby.

"Yes."

"That's O.K? Put it down to a couple of M.P.s. You know, I heard, that some wretched chap actually bought a book of bills off a waiter here."

"That's going too far," said Leo.
"Much too far," said Toby severely.

The other lunch was at San Frediano in the Fulham Road; trendy, crowded and noisy, mini-skirts and Mary Quant. Pippa and Wanda arrived together. Franco smiled a busy welcome. "I think we can find a place," and squeezed them into a corner table. Several people greeted Wanda.

"Hello, darling. What's new?"

"Not me, Nigel."

"My golly, he's a busy bee," added Wanda seating herself and looking around.

She was wearing a pale linen trouser suit, golden hair cascading over her shoulders, sunglasses hiding the cornflower blue eyes. Men eyed her, continuing their conversation. Pippa wore a black top, very short pink mini-skirt, PVC mac in her hand, her dark hair in a fringe under a black beret. A waiter eventually took their order.

"Something salady, I fancy. Pellegrino and lots of ice."

"How's the sweat-shop?" said Wanda.

"Sweaty. We've acquired a new young man."

"Any good?"

"I tried him, he'll learn."

Pippa lit a cigarette.

"Good joke, by the way. Tim asked who Kim Adrian was. Quentin had to explain."

"Very good joke. What did you say?"

"Nothing, of course. Vaguely winked at Q."

"You'd think," said Wanda, "that a shit-hot programme like Good Evening would have heard of Kim. Why did they ask?"

"Old Benno mentioned him."

"He would. Talking of Kim, he's got a new racket going, might even interest you", said Wanda. The waiter served two salads.

"What's Kim's thing?" said Pippa.

"It's called the Military Attaches Circuit," said Wanda. "He went to one of their parties, they all know each other, and he realised that most of them have good expense accounts, bugger all to do and an eye for the birds. Some of them, you know, from South America and Africa are quite dishy. Anyway, I thought it would make a change from the Saudis. Frankly I'm bored with burnouses."

Pippa laughed. "Screwing?"

"Not unless you want to."

"I don't get it. You mean they pay all that cash without screwing?"

"Well, it's like this," said Wanda. "They really only like screwing scrubbers but they want to be seen around town at embassy parties and so on with respectable dollies like us." They both laughed. "If we screw it's a bonus."

"Do you?" said Pippa.

"Hardly ever. I've got enough on my plate with Nikki."

"Who he?"

"Current. Super-rich, dishy, art dealer or something in Germany. Better still he owns an island in the Caribbean. We're off there soon."

"Sounds O.K.," said Pippa. "How do I join Kim's outfit?"

"Come along to one of his parties."

"Not good at orgies."

"No, darling, all very respectable. Chaps in suits from the City, politicos, the odd diplomat. You'd have to restrain yourself, knowing you."

"Thanks a lot."

"You're welcome. Isn't that a ghastly Yank phrase?"

Chapter Four

Simon spent the next week researching the Home Secretary. With Melanie's help he trawled the picture libraries, viewed newsreel clips, thumbed through political memoirs and press cuttings, groaned over pages of Hansard. It was a chore unrelieved by any spark of drama or scandal. On the plus side however he saw more of Pippa.

One afternoon after an alcoholic lunch in the club Simon said, "Viznews have sent over some stuff from the last election. Do you want to see it?"

"Might as well," said Pippa.

For twenty minutes they watched a balding, middle-aged man getting in and out of cars, walking with a fixed smile down suburban streets, talking awkwardly to housewives, uneasy in a pub, peering at a fruit stall and being followed aggressively by journalists. Finally the bored film editor said, "That's the lot. I'll take the cans back to despatch," and left.

Pippa turned to Simon in the gloom of the small stuffy viewing theatre. "He's a real crasher, isn't he?"

"What can we do about it?"

Pippa grinned. "There's something I can do," and moved her hand across to undo the zip on his trousers.

"Suppose the film editor returns?" said Simon weakly.

"Don't you enjoy it?"
"Yes."
"You don't?"
No, of course I do," said Simon flustered.
"Well then," said Pippa.

Two days later Simon wandered over to the club after watching the programme. Quentin had interviewed an ageing and rather grand American film star. She had replied to his first question by saying, "That sounds like one of those tired old familiar clichés about Hollywood." Quentin smiled, "Perhaps we could have one of those old familiar answers." She didn't try another putdown.

Toby had been engaged in his favourite occupation, baiting politicians. So probing had his interview become that the junior Minister resorted to calling Toby "Mr Inquisitor." It was a clever move. Toby grinned and relaxed his grip.

Quentin and Toby entered the club together and they joined Simon at the bar.

A few moments later Pippa appeared, friendly, affectionate. "I was looking for you," she said. "We're going to a party, aren't we, Q?"

"Of course."

"Am I invited," asked Simon.

"By me you are," said Pippa.

"Whose party?"

"Too many questions," said Quentin. "I've got a taxi waiting."

"Good luck, " said Toby knowingly.

The taxi took them to a mews house off Cavendish Street. The door was opened by an out-of-work actor who beamed at Quentin and Pippa and nodded faintly to Simon. "Lovely people, give me your coats. You know the way." The rippling hum of conversation came from above. At the top of the stairs stood Kim Adrian.

At forty-five he was at the height of his ambiguous career. Best described by that old-fashioned but apt phrase, "a man about town," he had made London his town and he was certainly about it. He turned up everywhere: First Nights, Embassy receptions, the Peers Dining Room at the House of Lords, private parties in Belgravia and not so private parties in Chelsea, the Savoy Grill, the Beefsteak and even occasionally the Spanish Garden. No one seemed to know his background, he had indeed risen without trace. But once accepted he moved easily in whatever world he found himself.

Another out-of-work actor appeared with a tray of drinks. Quentin slid into the crowd and Pippa took Simon's arm. It was the sort of party which reflected Kim's interests, the Establishment mixing with smart Bohemia. M.P.s, City directors, diplomats felt safe mingling with the more respectable actors and actresses, broadsheet editors, fashionable artists and sober authors. The young women were carefully chosen; Kim never made the mistake of randomly mixing business with pleasure.

Pippa scanned the crowd.

"She said she'd be here."

"Who?"

"Someone special. Over there." She guided Simon to where a young woman and an older man were talking intimately.

"Darling."

The young woman who turned round completely captivated Simon. Wanda was looking at her best in a short summer dress displaying her long slender legs. Asked once by an inquisitive man about her inside leg measurement she had replied coolly, "Thirty-six inches, if you must know, but thirty-seven if I'm in a good mood."

"Hi, Pippa. I don't think you know Colonel Carlos," adding, "of the Brazilian Air Force. Planes, you know. He flies through the air with the greatest of ease, don't you, darling?" The lean, handsome aviator smiled and bowed. "And who are you?" said Wanda amiably to Simon. Pippa introduced them.

"Like me, darling, he slaves for your old dad."

"Poor sod," said Wanda. "Let's have some more champagne. I really think Kim might splash out a bit on vintage stuff, this is pure Jackson Frères."

"Who he, sweetie?"

"Pooter, favourite book."

"Didn't know you had time for reading."

"Simon, it is Simon, isn't it?" said Wanda, "you must keep this girl on a tight rein, she can be difficult." The colonel beamed at the allusion to horses.

Later in the evening Quentin beckoned to Pippa and Simon and they followed him into a smallish room, part study, library and office; opulent

Wanda

furniture added a flavour of the boudoir. Kim was leaning against a bookcase smoking a cigarette. He motioned them to deep armchairs. "Quentin has told me about this somewhat bizarre idea of yours. I really don't know ... ah, there she is."

Wanda strolled into the room and Kim's world-weary face lightened. "All chums," said Wanda taking a window seat. When Kim had explained rather diffidently she laughed, looking at each of them.

"What a hoot! Dear old George Worthington of all people. Now if it was Jack or even Duncan I could understand. But George, a life of blameless tedium. I've known him for years. I remember the first time he came down to stay at Chilton, I was about sixteen and we went for a walk after lunch and he steered me into the boathouse and I thought here goes but all he did was rabbit on about boats."

"I know, darling," said Kim, "but they think if you were to…"

"Go to bed with George. You must be joking."

"No, darling," said Kim patiently, "nothing like that. All they suggest is that you have a chat with the old boy occasionally on the off chance that he lets slip some indiscretion or something. Isn't that right?"

"Sort of," said Quentin.

"Shop old George," said Wanda. "Whatever next. You're all a bit bonkers if you ask me. Comes of working in television. Is this some delicious plot of my clever father?"

"No, darling," said Quentin, "Just fishing."

"Some catch."

"But you will give it a try," said Pippa.

"Give anything a try, darling," said Wanda. "Always have, that's my trouble. Now, back to the aviator."

The following week they began filming, starting with some M.Ps who knew the Home Secretary. They were a tiresome lot who changed the filming times, altered the questions, made party points and queried the fees.

Simon was then sent to sound out Old Benno. The train from Charing Cross pottered along ancient tracks into deepest Sussex. Benno was waiting on the platform and they drove off in his old Mini. He talked continuously, often driving on the pavement and once over part of a traffic island. The local policeman waved indulgently.

"Nice chap," said Benno, "beds the village school mistress. His wife's bound to find out."

In the comfortable thatched cottage Mrs Benno was charmingly vague. "So you're the new editor of Panorama?"

"No, darling, Simon's from Good Evening."

"Who else is coming?"

"Just John and that Canadian, you remember we met in Toronto."

"Very likely."

Lunch was convivial, gossipy, vegetarian for the Bennos, ham salad and light ale for the others. Benno asked Simon how he was getting on with the Home Secretary.

"Not very well."

"Did you contact Kim Adrian?"

"Quentin took us to one of his parties."

John looked intrigued. "You're not telling me that old George Worthington was at one of Kim's parties?"

Benno chuckled. "John writes for "Private Eye". Scandal is their quiddity."

"You can talk, Benno."

"Touché, dear boy. I merely suggested that no one could be as pure white as our Home Secretary and perhaps unholy Kim might know where the bodies are buried."

"Did he?" asked John.

"He's looking into it," said Simon, adding, "with someone called Wanda Haddon."

"Don't know her," said Benno.

"I've heard Nigel mention her," said John. "It all sounds rather interesting, the Home Secretary, Kim Adrian and the Wanda girl."

"What did I tell you," said Benno, pleased with himself.

Mrs Benno was serving some delicious apple pie. "This Kim person, darling. Was he someone you knew in your Indian days?"

"No, darling, I don't think you've met him."

Later, when she was in the kitchen, Benno said, "Dear Meg, she does rather confuse people. Recently at a party she was introduced to Vidal Sassoon and she said to him that she was afraid that she hadn't read his latest novel. Mistook him for Gore."

After lunch Benno led them on a long walk over the summer countryside, through aromatic hop fields, apple-heavy orchards and shadowed woods. He talked most of the time, a stimulating mixture of anecdote, despairing comment and a wryly amusing demonology of his contemporaries. At one point John took over the conversation but, unused to the corrugated paths, he slipped into a dry ditch and reverted to silence. After all, thought Simon, we have come all this way to listen to Benno.

A few days later in the club Hilda button-holed Tim. "How is the Foreign Secretary documentary coming along?"

"Home Secretary, Hilda."

"That's what I said. You'll be glad to know the chairman is taking a personal interest. Is Toby coping?"

"Yes. They filmed Benno yesterday."

"Good. None of his wicked stories, I trust. You must be ruthless with the editing. I shall see a rough-cut of course but I don't want any slip-ups. Remember the Buggins business." Tim remembered. Alf Buggins, an unknown Labour M.P. had been included in a programme about a housing scandal. Somehow he had been confused with a dodgy Tory M.P. called Baggins. Buggins had sued and walked off with a comfortable sum.

"And another thing," said Hilda. She suddenly spied Ginger Ruddle.

"What other thing?" asked Tim.

"What do you mean?" said Hilda.

"You said another thing."

"What other thing?"

"The other thing you meant to say," said Tim patiently.

"What *are* you talking about?" barked Hilda moving towards Ginger.

"Nothing..." said Tim retreating to the bar.

"Ruddle." Ginger approached Hilda reluctantly, pint glass in hand. "What's all this I hear about you wanting to do a film on Dylan Thomas?"

"Well…"

"Don't waffle like Tim. Make yourself clear. You should know that Dylan Thomas is not a person I have ever approved of and you'll find it hard to convince me. Nor do I want you wandering about all over Wales. I remember Emlyn Williams once telling me that the natives can be quite hostile. I'm sure he wasn't joking either."

"It's actually about his time in London."

"I seem to remember," said Hilda severely, "that he worked for the BBC at some time. I need not remind you that we do not give the BBC gratuitous favours. In their own way admittedly they do some nice little things, animal programmes, Blue Peter and the like. But I certainly don't expect you to waste time watching them."

"No, it's not particularly about the BBC," said Ginger evasively.

"Speak to H-P. He's often talking about the London Welsh, probably a choir or something. As I recall Thomas came to a bad end so we don't want any of that." She drank her gin. "By and large,

Ruddle, I am of course in favour of poetry. Remember the quotation, 'Three sacred things, poets, groves and kings.' Although," she added moving away, "I'm not entirely sure about groves."

Tim regained the Good Evening group. "Leo, Hilda's on about your doc."

"She suggested the other day that I use Randolph," said Leo.

"Good God, didn't she see him recently on Panorama singing 'Bless 'em all'?"

Simon sat eating a sausage roll his eyes on Pippa. Her behaviour of ignoring him one day and recreating their intimacy the next was beyond his experience or comprehension, leaving him simultaneously excited and frustrated. She caught his glance and moved across to the adjacent chair. "Doing anything this evening?"

Simon had intended to visit his parents. "No. Another party?"

"Supper with a chum. See you after the prog."

Passing through the lobby Simon gave the usual greeting to Wendy. She stared back stonily. "You're all shits." She busied herself with some papers. He reported this to Toby. "Oh, God, Leo's at it again."

In the office H-P was confronting a peevish Ginger.

"Nor, I gather, is Hilda happy with the idea. I had the misfortune to meet Dylan and he was both drunk and obscene."

"What's that got to do with his poetry?"

"It's not the poetry apparently that you are concentrating on."

"What do you mean?" said Ginger.

"Friends of mine at B.H. tell me that you intend filming in the George.

"So what?" said Ginger scratching his beard.

"All you'll get there will be disreputable stories of his drinking habits. He was a disgrace to Wales."

"What about Lloyd George?"

"What about him?"

"Wasn't he a disgrace to Wales? All that screwing."

"Not many people knew at the time."

"The girls he screwed knew all right," said Ginger.

H-P saw that the argument couldn't be won at that level. He moved towards the door.

"All I can say is that such a programme will not add to the reputation of Good Evening."

As the door closed Ginger farted crisply.

"You're a crude sort of bugger, aren't you?" said Tim.

"Yes," said Ginger.

In the club that evening Pippa put her arm round Simon and said, "Time to go." In the taxi it was agreeably clear to him that she was in an affectionate mood although reluctant to say who they were going to meet.

Nick's Bistro was one of the many popular eating places which had sprung up in the Sixties. It was small, hot, stuffy, scruffy and uncomfortable; the food was not particularly good, there was loud music and the service was appalling. Young people loved it.

Pippa was greeted by a bearded young man, shirtless, in torn jeans. Simon surmised that he might be Nick. They were shown to a table mercifully in an alcove. Plates and glasses of previous customers were still in place; a red candle guttered over a check tablecloth.

"Makes a change from San Fred," said Pippa waving to a girl wearing deep eye-shadow and white lipstick.

Wanda came through the door smiling, carefree, mini-skirted with a plastic handbag over her shoulder which dislodged a bread basket from one of the tables she passed. "Pip, darling, isn't this hell? And the nice researcher, Simon, too. Haven't been here for yonks. Anyone around?"

"It's the only place one can have a private chat," said Pippa. "Can't be overheard in this din."

After a while Nick handed them a piece of cardboard with purple writing. "What do you think the savoury pancakes are like?" said Wanda.

"I don't," said Pippa.

"Let's have some onion soup."

"Wine?" asked Nick.

"As long as it's not Spanish burgundy," said Wanda.

Simon studied her, spell-bound once again. She wore no eye-shadow, no make-up on the pearl skin. Was it the cheek bones which gave her a faintly oriental look; not the golden hair and blue eyes. He noticed her small pointed breasts, slender body, bare sunburnt arms, no jewellery.

"Haven't seen you since Kim's party", said Wanda "all that plotting or whatever. You'd think I was ... who was it?"

"Mata Hari," said Pippa.

"Quite likely. Reminds me I was once given a spy book with a rather super title, *Madonna of the Sleeping Cars*. Never read it but it's rather me, don't you think?"

"Spot on. Pity they don't run the Orient Express, you'd have a ball."

"Hold on," said Wanda, "I once got on something called the Orient Express at the Gare de l'Est. It said it was going to Damascus, I read the board on the carriage. But it certainly wasn't sinister or glamorous."

"Where were you going?" asked Pippa.

"Vienna. Home from school."

"Didn't know you lived in Vienna."

"My father was at the Embassy briefly. Anyway you and I had parted company by then. Remember, I'd just been turfed out of some school or other."

"Poor old maths master went too as I recall." said Pippa.

"I thought he taught geography. He certainly taught me one or two things."

"Sure it wasn't the other way round?"

"Not according to his wife," said Wanda. They both laughed.

"What went on in Vienna?" asked Pippa.

"Quite a lot, come to think of it." Wanda sipped some wine. "But I doubt if Simon wants to hear about girls' goings-on."

"Goings-off," said Pippa.

"Yes, I do," said Simon.

"Well," said Wanda lighting a cigarette, "Vienna in 1953 was still a bit battered but a blissful city really. I thought so at that age. The old boy was working and mama was doing food parcels for spies or something and I was left in the care of the assistant military attaché, a rather dishy chap called Rupert something who wore a sort of chain mail on his blues, all very romantic. So we knocked about Vienna, shopping in the Karnerstrasse and picnicking in the Lainzers Tiergarten, giving the left-overs to the monkeys. I was of course crazy about Orson Welles and we kept going on the big wheel in the Prater. The dear lad even got permission for us to go down the sewers, they're just like the movie, no smell, very exciting." She sipped some more wine. "Are you asleep, Pip? Have a pudding or something."

"Go on," said Simon.

"Yes, well, one afternoon we'd been looking round the Hofberg or Schonbrunn or somewhere and he could see I was bored stupid, so we went back to his flat on the Parkring and he just seduced me. Dead easy really because I longed for it. But when I told him I was fifteen the poor pongo had a fit, career in ruins, court martial, shot at dawn or 'you know what to do, Cavendish,' all that stuff. Would I tell my father? I said I jolly well would if he didn't go on seducing me. So that was fun, although I think he was a wee bit relieved to be posted away a few weeks later."

"Hadn't heard that before," said Pippa. "I thought you were raped in the loo on Basle station."

"That too probably. So back to boring old England to be chucked out of several schools. Didn't we meet up again in one of them?"

"I never knew about Vienna," said Pippa. "Funny about the chap being a military attaché."

"Yes, it is rather. Know anything about Roumania?"

"Why?"

"Naval attaché."

"Bit heavy."

Wanda grinned at Simon. "Terrible tart. Do you disapprove?"

"Good God, no. I only wish I was a military whatever."

"I call that rather sweet, Pip, don't you?"

"Sort of."

"Don't be so cool, darling. After all you started me off on the slippery slope."

"When? Where? I don't remember."

"Yes, you do. We were drinking in the Spanish Garden with some frightful shit you'd met at one of Beecher's parties and he introduced me to Kim."

"Well, I never, said Pippa. "I'd forgotten that. I must say you've been jolly successful."

"Haven't I just," said Wanda. "I think I fancy a pudding".

Over coffee Pippa said casually, "Seen anything of George W. lately?"

"Oh, him. Met him briefly at the American Embassy. He called me 'dear girl', and asked me to lunch at Cunningham's."

"Better go," said Pippa.

"Must I?"

"Might help."

"Mata Hari stuff?"

"Sort of," said Pippa.

On the way home in the taxi she said to Simon, "I think you're smitten."

"What an odd word."

"Are you?"

"Not really."

"Balls," said Pippa, "you can't take your eyes off her."

"Well…"

"Beautiful?"

"Yes."

"Sexy?"

"Yes"

"Amusing?"

"Yes"

"So."

"What I don't understand," said Simon, "is why she does, well, what she does."

"Don't be dim."

"Well…"

"Look, I remember her saying, quite candid as always, that being completely uneducated she could only be bunged into some lousy job with her father's influence - like those dollies at Lime Grove, all sprogs with well-known fathers. Modelling - all right for a few, Barbara Goalen, Anne Gunning, but the rag trade is hell. What else? No, sweetie, being a high-class hooker isn't all fun and games but for someone with Wanda's temperament it's a damn sight less aggers than some nine to five slog. And it's not exactly badly paid. You and I work for her father for a measly two thousand a year - she probably makes that in a month."

"Could you do it?" said Simon.

"Dunno. Why not?." Pippa grinned, "But I tell you now we're on the subject what I *could* do," leaning down to Simon. "Haven't done it in a taxi for ages."

"Christ, no," said Simon unavailingly.

Chapter Five

Next day, after the morning meeting, Tim asked Simon, "Can you help out on the programme today, we're a bit short-handed?"

"What's to do?"

"Mad professor, I'm afraid. H-P's got hold of someone who wants to build a dam across the Channel to change the weather. He's coming down from Nottingham."

When Simon returned to his office he found Toby reading the *Daily Express*.

"Hickey," said Toby pointing. "Isn't this your glorious bird?"

The picture taken at a reception at the American embassy showed Wanda talking to the ambassador and the Home Secretary with a caption "Tycoon's daughter promotes special relationship at a garden party…"

"Can we use the picture?" asked Simon.

"You bet. If there's any bother ask for Donald, I know him."

In the club at lunchtime Hilda was talking to H-P.

"I'm not at all happy about this idea of Ruddle's. Has he consulted you?"

"I should hardly call it consultation. He was most offensive when I suggested that the idea was not one the Welsh would approve of."

"What's it got to do with the Welsh?" said Hilda scanning the bar for likely victims.

"Swansea, Hilda. Born and brought up there if not exactly a tribute to that fine city."

"I understood the Home Secretary is a West Country man."

"The Home Secretary?"

"Yes, yes. George Worthington has agreed to do the profile."

"I thought…"

"There was the usual muddle. Ruddle wanted to do a documentary about Dylan Thomas of all people. Most unsuitable, I told him, there's quite enough drinking around here without glorifying it. So I came up with the idea of the Home Secretary."

"Excellent," said H-P.

"And what are you doing this evening?"

"Brilliant engineer, Hilda. Very advanced ideas about the weather."

"That reminds me," said Hilda making a bee-line for Simon. "I must have a word with Collins the new catering manager."

After lunch Simon reported to H-P's office; he almost felt obliged to salute. "Ah, young Simon, how are you enjoying life on this programme?"

"I think…"

"Most young men would give their eye teeth to work here. Nothing like a good grounding in the grammar of television. True, lucid, brief, one, two, three, the secret of good television. What is our real goal?"

"Well…"

H-P

"Excellence. The grail we all seek and seldom achieve..." H-P paused, almost lost for words in the prospect of a Television Society Silver Medal. "But we mustn't day-dream, Laddie." He handed Simon a photo-copied article from the *Engineer's Weekly*. "This is Professor Emden's thesis. We shall require footage of the Channel and a diagram of the barrier. Get cracking."

Simon returned to Toby's office. "How do I get a diagram done?"

"There's a bloke who lives round the corner," said Toby. "He does it by hand, and he's Austrian so make sure he knows exactly what you want. He did us a map of India recently and failed to mark in Pakistan. We had all the local shop keepers on the blower."

Later H-P handed him a long intro. "Get this typed out on the Jumbo and take the diagram up to the studio." He relaxed in his chair and lit his pipe.

"We live in an age of change. I see a new spirit abroad..." he began.

And for once in his garrulous life H-P spoke more prophetically than he knew. The decade that was just beginning would indeed bring amazing changes. In years to come old men in their clubs would remark resentfully, "It all began to go wrong in the Sixties, you know."

Some time later Simon collected the diagram from the front desk in the lobby. Wendy was on duty; all the phones were ringing. "Make yourself useful," she said shortly. Simon picked up the nearest phone. A man's voice said, "Hello, sweetie, how about this evening?"

"It's not Wendy," said Simon stupidly. "Is that Leo?"

"For Christ's sake," said Leo, ringing off.

"That was Leo."

"Was it?" said Wendy frostily.

Ziggy had the lift gates open. "Good evening, squire, the fourth, I trust?" Ziggy fished around in his pocket and produced a ring. "When I say semi-precious stone I don't mean it's not very precious. It's actually an engagement ring that's been in my family for, well, quite a long time."

"Not really, Ziggy."

"A young man like you never knows when he'll need an engagement ring."

"Too true."

In the studio the floor manager groaned when he saw the three cards of H-P's intro. "One of these days I'll quite likely put the bloody cards on the camera in the wrong order and serve the silly sod right. Which way up is this stupid diagram?"

'Intros' for Good Evening often bordered on the eccentric. The programme was obsessed with anniversaries and one such intro began, 'Today Rasputin would have been eighty-nine had he lived...'

Later Simon was in Toby's office when Wendy rang to say that Professor Someone-or-other had arrived. She was at the front desk applying lipstick and nodded Simon towards a small, neat, balding middle-aged man. "There's your dotty professor."

Flustered, Simon said, "I'm sorry…"

"Perhaps you are sorry that I'm not a dotty professor." They were the precise tones of High Table.

In hospitality Professor Emden accepted a whiskey and soda. "Very interesting idea, the Channel Barrier," said Simon.

The professor put down his glass. "Young man, you may also be interested to know that on my way down here in the train I re-checked my calculations and found that in no way can my scheme work. It will need a great deal more research. It is in fact an idea whose time, you might say, has not yet come." He looked at Simon with a weary tolerance reminiscent of tutorials at Oxford during an ill-prepared essay.

"I think," said Simon, "I'd better make a phone call," and he slipped into the next room.

H-P took the news with surprising nonchalance. "Stupid fellow. I've met this kind of don before, too much time in the ivory tower and not enough in the engine-room. Don't worry, I shall play devil's advocate, put his case and let him try and counter it. Lively stuff, I fancy. Keep him happy, laddie, until I arrive."

The floor manager received the new one-card intro with wry amusement. "Cock-up time, is it?"

Simon poured himself a large drink and settled down to watch the programme.

H-P skilfully extracted an interview from a somewhat bewildered professor. To millions of viewers busy with children, meals, evening papers and the usual domestic distractions it was merely the 'telly'. All one to them unless the screen suddenly went blank and their regular drug was withdrawn. The TV bosses had already spotted that what the public most wanted was the same programme at the same time as often as possible - the "soap-opera". Good Evening was a wonderful up-market 'soap'. Now only the drinkers in hospitality spotted the deception and showed their amusement.

Simon began to notice that H-P had a mild idiosyncrasy: his hands conveyed a different meaning to his words. If he said, "bring together" he would spread his hands apart; "open out" would close them. "There are two points" was indicated with three fingers. Mention of "level" caused a circular motion of the hands. It was a bizarre body language.

A little later Hilda sailed unsteadily into hospitality. "Interesting idea, Channel Tunnel," she remarked genially to a now totally bewildered professor, and then bore down on Tim. "I thought that I'd made it clear that I disapproved of Ruddle's idea about the Thomas film."

"Well…"

"As I said to him in the club I am not in any way against poets and poetry. Some of them, the English ones, have written very nice little verses. I know that one or two had unstable private lives but that can't be helped, writing poetry is a risky business for earning a living."

"I think…"

"Don't interrupt. Where was I? It's the subject matter I'm not entirely happy about. What with Vietnam and Algeria people don't want to be reminded of war. Although I must say the Great War produced better poets than the last one. Different sort of war. I remember Douglas Haig telling me that despite being abroad he was quite comfortable in his chateau." She looked at Tim. "I'm old enough, you know, to recall the announcement of the death of Rupert Brooke. The nation was stunned. Winston wrote a wonderful piece in *The Times*."

"Perhaps…"

"Do be quiet. To get back to the point, I'm almost sure that Edward Thomas was killed later on, 1917, I fancy. A very fine poet, a nature poet they called him. But this is not really the time…"

"Hilda!"

"What is it for Heaven's sake?"

"Nothing," said Tim taking her glass.

Next morning in Toby's office Simon referred to the dotty professor fiasco.

"Nothing to worry about," said Toby fiddling with a paper clip. "Wait until you get stuck with film people. Worst occasion was an American director, big shot with a new epic on release. When I asked him on air the first question he replied, 'Well, I reckon ... blah, blah, blah.' I thought he was nervous so I asked him another. He replied, 'blah, blah' again. It turned out that he thought we were doing a rehearsal. Poor sod nearly passed out." Toby smiled grimly. "Then there was the very famous film star so dim that not only did he want the questions written down beforehand but also the flipping answers. Dear lad, you don't know the half."

He paused, abandoning the paper clip. "Thing about interviewing is that nearly everyone thinks he can do it - and often does. Anyone *can* read a list of questions off a clipboard. The secret, if there is one, is to listen to the answers and pop in supplementary questions, preferably short ones, it gives the interviewee less time to think. Also if you can, try holding the pause, it prompts the other chap to carry on talking. If only they knew, the best way to get out of a sticky interview is to ask the *interviewer* a question - it brings the whole thing to a halt." He retrieved the paper clip. "I'm talking too bloody much. Better go and see what's going on."

In his office Tim fired the popgun and said, "Outing for you, Simon. *Private Eye* lunch. Apparently you met someone at Benno's."

"What can I tell them?"

"Anything you like."

He found the pub in Soho, in the Sixties a lively ethnic mixture of wine shops, charcuteries, bakeries, cafes and inexpensive restaurants; before the coming of the sordid and flashy strip clubs. The saloon bar was sparsely furnished with wooden tables and chairs, a fruit machine, lino on the floor. A large man sat behind the bar reading the racing pages of the *Evening Standard*. He glanced up at Simon. "What the hell do you want?"

"I thought that *Private Eye*…"

"Up there," said the man with a jerk of his thumb, returning to his paper.

The upstairs room had some similar old wooden chairs and a long table on which were bottles of wine and Apollinaris water. The editor introduced him to those present: a disreputable MP, a woman columnist, a TV 'personality' and several of the *Eye* staff writers. Steak and chips was followed by apple pie and cheddar, all served slapdash by the landlord.

"Richard, this wine, worse than usual."

"I know, Bron."

Conversation varied between intimate chats and general badinage up and down the table. The editor, sipping Apollinaris water, presided at one end, mostly listening with his habitual wry smile; Nigel held more boisterous court at the other end. The woman columnist sitting next to Simon asked him what he did, nodded and lost interest. After the M.P. had relayed the latest gossip about fellow Members the editor turned to Simon. "John said something about a profile you're doing of George Worthington.

"Yes."

"He mentioned Kim Adrian."

"Surely not together," said the M.P.

"And," added the editor, "Wanda Haddon."

"Not possible," said the M.P. involuntarily taking a swig of wine and wincing. The editor called casually down the table. "Nigel, Wanda Haddon, do you know her?"

"Of course I do. Old Farrier's daughter and one of Kim Adrian's beauties."

"George Worthington, any connection?"

"Unbelievable," said the M.P.

"Now you mention it," said Nigel, "I have seen them hobnobbing at one or two embassy do's."

"I saw them at Cunningham's the other lunchtime," said the woman columnist.

"Holding hands?"

"Not exactly."

"Well, good for old George," said the M.P.

"Does Farrier *know* about his daughter?" asked the editor.

"Shouldn't think he cares," said Nigel, "considering his own larks."

"I heard that White's had their own brothel in South Kensington," said the M.P. "There's a story that a new unbriefed inspector raided the place and found himself back on point duty." The editor smiled his world-weary smile.

On Saturday at a loose end, Simon decided to go into the studios to catch up on some work, sift cuttings and type out notes. Kitty was on the front desk reading a newspaper. "What on earth brings you in? Are they paying you overtime?"

"I wanted to see you."

"A likely story. By the way, you can tell that creepy Leo he's upsetting Wendy. I won't have it. He even made a pass at me when I was first here."

"What did you do?"

"I didn't," said Kitty, adding casually, "You're not the only one."

Wondering what she meant Simon entered the empty cottage through Ginger's office littered with old newspapers, magazines and cans of film. On the steps of the stairs he was suddenly checked by the voice of Melanie, pleading. "No, please, Toby, don't, please."

"Get over the desk." Toby's voice was harsh, unfamiliar. Simon stood, disturbed, aroused. "Don't, please." Was the anguish now tinged with a note of compliance? As a rhythmic moaning began Simon retreated, more disturbed than aroused.

That afternoon in bed with Pippa he said, "You know, I think that Toby is screwing little Melanie."

"What do you mean, you think?"

Simon told her. "Of course he was, so what?"

"I didn't think…"

"Darling, you are the most naive chump I've ever come across." She stroked his thigh.

A little later Simon said softly, "I love you."

"No, you don't."

"Do you love me?"

"Good God, no."

"Why not?"

"Because ... oh, for Christ's sake let's not confuse screwing with hearts and flowers."

"Don't you love me a little bit?" said Simon with the hopelessness of youth.

"Look," said Pippa caressing him, "I like you, isn't that enough? Now let's try a super new idea I've learnt. It's called the Tired Duke, Ugly Duchess

Position. You lie on your back and I lie on my back on top of you."

"Jesus," said Simon, "I may be a chump but I'm not a contortionist."

"Oh, come on," said Pippa rolling him over.

It was *Private Eye* unsurprisingly which first made a direct reference to the matter. A brief paragraph in 'Grovel' stated: *George 'Worthy' Worthington, Britain's dullest Home Secretary since Chuter Ede may not agree with homosexual law reform but is apparently not averse to hobnobbing with golden bombshell, Wanda Haddon, 'model' daughter of TV tycoon Lord Farrier. Could Uganda be on the agenda?*

In Fleet Street the editor of the great newspaper noticed the item. "Anything in this, Donald?"

"Not a lot. Why?"

"The Old Man's been on from Jamaica. He saw the embassy party picture and he's fallen out with Farrier over something. He also wants a cabinet reshuffle. Could we run with this?"

"I'll get on to Kim Adrian, he owes me one."

"Right away."

"O. K."

Toby read the item out to Pippa and Leo. "Good girl," said Pippa.

"When am I going to meet this gorgeous Wanda?" said Leo.

"There's a new barmaid in the club," said Toby.

"Very funny," said Leo leaving the room.

Wanda read it, having a drink in Claridges with her current boy-friend, Nikki, and barely gave it a thought. They were discussing a holiday on his island near Martinique.

Kim Adrian, smoking a Passing Cloud after breakfast, read it with interest, adding yet another skein to the web of intrigue which, unlike a spider, he wove mainly to amuse himself. Fantasy played a large part in the life of Kim Adrian.

Contentedly unaware of this growing interest in him George Worthington was once again having his fortnightly lunch with his old school friend at the Oxford and Cambridge club. He had not even heard of the relatively new magazine, *Private Eye*, and it fell to someone at a nearby table, a cheeky Labour backbencher, to draw his attention to the item.
"Living it up a bit, George, eh?"
"What are you talking about?"
 He was shown the paragraph. "Good Heavens, what a lot of rubbish," said the Home Secretary. "I've known the young girl since she was at school with one of my daughters. Archie Farrier is not exactly my type but we've been friends for years. Where do rags like this get all their nonsense? And why on earth should I want to talk to her about Uganda?"

He turned back to the brown Windsor soup and reminiscences of the old days. It was only later over coffee that surprise and mild irritation were replaced by an absurd twinge of self-esteem. All his life in the deep recesses of his honourable soul he had been aware that despite his First in History, his war time O.B.E., his political achievements, he was in fact a very ordinary person to whom no exciting, romantic, dangerous or scandalous event would ever happen. Now at the age of fifty-two some rag was suggesting that he was having an affair with a twenty-five year old friend of the family. It was ridiculous; it was disturbing.

"I *said*, George, do you know what happened to Freddie Allgood. I don't think you are listening."

"Sorry, Henry, I was miles away. Freddie Allgood..."

Interlude

In the drab offices of MI5 in Northumberland Avenue a routine meeting was drawing to a close.

"Any other business," asked the Director. He was a former policeman more at home with dubious confessions and regular "searches" than the new world of computers and electronic surveillance.

"We have had an anonymous denunciation," said the Section Head. The Director sighed. More time-wasting.

"You know we don't treat them seriously. Last time, if I remember, it was against the Archbishop of Canterbury".

"Who is it now?"

The Section Head paused, looked embarrassed and mumbled, "It's against Sir Anthony Blunt."

The Director looked at him pityingly. "I do not begin to understand why you are wasting our time. Can you think of anyone less likely to be a foreign agent than the Surveyor of the Queen's Pictures? I ask you."

"No."

"Well, then. In future I think that you should disregard all A.D.s"

"Very good."

"Anything else?"

The Deputy Director cleared his throat. "A matter has arisen, sir."

"Yes." His Deputy was always prolonging meetings, had he nothing better to do?

"Which perhaps I shouldn't bring up at an open meeting."

"Well, it seems you have now, Watson." He wished his Deputy was not called Watson, it seemed to amuse junior members of staff.

"Well, sir, it concerns the Home Secretary."

"Everything does, Watson, as well you know."

"No sir, I mean it concerns him personally."

There was a general ripple of interest round the table. "How do you mean?" Was the man off his head? Only recently he had been found wandering round the offices in dark glasses, bumping into furniture.

The Deputy Director consulted some notes. "It has come to our notice that the subject under discussion, to wit the Secretary of State, has been observed associating intimately with a person known to the police." Stunned silence. The Director suddenly felt unwell. Visions of press headlines, very early retirement, a vanished knighthood, flitted before his eyes. "Who on earth are you talking about?"

"A young woman called Lady Alice Haddon."

A puzzled murmur. Then one of the more social Section Heads said, "Surely she's the daughter of the Earl Farrier?"

"That is correct."

"How can she be known to the police?" said the Director, recovering himself.

"She is known for giving sexual favours in return for money."

"Are you suggesting that she is a prostitute?"

"I think, sir, the more accurate term now is call-girl."

"Well, whatever she is, it all sounds astonishing. Do you mean that the Home Secretary is, er, consorting with this girl?"

"Not exactly consorting."

"Well, what was he doing?"

"He was observed, as I have said, in several intimate situations."

"Such as?" said the Director.

"On two occasions in the Savoy Hotel."

"You mean in a bedroom?"

"Not exactly. Although the Home Secretary is known to use the Savoy after late night sittings in the House."

The Director looked sternly at his Deputy. "I think, Watson, that you are indulging in very wild and irresponsible conjecture. The behaviour of the S. of S. would appear to be at best completely above board; at worst a trifle indiscreet."

The Deputy Director ploughed on with his notes. "The problem, sir, is that the lady concerned is also thought to consort with Military Attachés of Iron Curtain countries."

The Director felt faint again. "Are you sure?"

"Yes, sir. One of our agents posing as the Bulgarian Air Attaché tried her out, as it were."

"Good heavens, who authorised that?"

"I did, sir."

"How, er, much was paid?"

"Two hundred pounds."

Gasps and indrawing of breath round the table. The Director steadied himself. "How did this come to our notice in the first place?"

"Information received and subsequent telephone calls arranging meetings."

A slight stir in the room. Telephone calls usually hinted at suspicious activities in the secret world.

"How did we know about the calls?" asked the Director.

"We put on a tap, sir," said the Deputy briskly.

A detonating silence in the room.

Finally, the Director spoke in slow, hushed, tones. "You put a tap on the private phone of the Home Secretary?"

"We considered it in the national interest."

More hushed tones. "Are you aware, Watson, that you require a red folder to put on a tap?"

"Yes, sir."

"And from whom do you get that permit?"

There was a pause. "From the Home Secretary," said the Deputy reflectively.

The Director took one of his pills. Sometimes he thought he had angina, at other times merely indigestion. "Gentlemen," he said, causing mild surprise because he had never called them that before, "what we have just heard is to be classified Most Secret and the minutes of this meeting are to be shredded…"

"A point, Director," broke in the Deputy.

"Yes, yes, what is it?"

"May I remind you that any shredding requires a green folder?"

"Very well," said the Director impatiently.

"And the latest amendment HD/61/571329 now requires the authorisation of the Home Secretary."

"Elementary, my dear Watson," murmured the junior member.

High up in a tall, plain building in Cork Street, off Piccadilly, in a sound-proof, bug-proof, overheated, under furnished room the Director of MI6 was at his desk. His 'In' tray and his 'Out' tray were empty, his telephone was silent, his telex machine quiescent; he was reading the latest James Bond novel. He had just reached one of many repetitively violent or erotic incidents when his intercom buzzed discreetly. "The Deputy Director would like to see you, sir," said his Roedean secretary.

Reluctantly he put down the novel, carefully marking the place with a Most Secret sticker, the only loose piece of paper on his desk. "All right, Miss Maresfield." They were traditionally formal in MI6, rather unlike Bond, he noticed.

A thin, bald, bespectacled man entered without knocking and approached the desk.

"Yes, Carruthers." He wished his Deputy had not been called Carruthers because he understood that for some reason jokes about the Secret Service were associated with the name. What's more, he was a Wykehamist. Sir Roderick had been at Eton.

"A rather delicate matter, Sir Roderick," said Carruthers. The Director beckoned him to a seat genially; he had only recently got his K.C.M.G. and was pleased to hear the title used. In the bad old days he understood that some irreverent members of MI6 (long since defected) had addressed the

Director as 'Chief'. "By the way," he said, "do you happen to have read this James Bond stuff?"

"I do not," said Carruthers.

"Just wondered."

Sir Roderick was somewhat out of touch with recent trends, he had been "Our Man in Ulan Bator" for five years. In fact that was one of the reasons for his rather surprise appointment, a general disenchantment with Whitehall bureaucrats after the Burgess-Maclean scandal. "Bring a fieldman in" someone had said at a Cabinet meeting as though he knew what he was talking about. And Sir Roderick had been at school with the Prime Minister.

"The situation," said Carruthers, "is that our man (he almost said "mole") in MI5 reports that they are sitting on what he considers to be a dangerous security problem."

"Ah."

"And the delicate point I referred to is that it concerns the Home Secretary."

"Well," said Sir Roderick glad to be clear about one thing, "MI5 is his bailiwick after all."

"No, Sir Roderick, I mean that the Home Secretary is himself the security risk." The Director took this badly. "Good God, man, do you mean George Worthington?"

"He is the Home Secretary."

"But how on earth...?"

"To put it concisely, Sir Roderick, the Home Secretary is carrying on a friendship with a known call-girl."

"Do you mean sleeping with her?"

"We are not sure."

"Well, then, what's wrong with that? Most of us have at one time or other had, shall we say, Bohemian friends, haven't we?"

"I have not."

"No, I suppose not. But what's all this got to do with the department? Surely it's an internal affair, er, matter, for the Home Office."

"This woman," said Carruthers, "is apparently also consorting with diplomats from countries behind the Iron Curtain."

Sir Roderick was plainly taken aback.

"Consorting? Consorting? Don't know the word. Does it mean…?"

"Yes, it does."

"That's bad. What do we know about this, er, call-girl? Lady of the Night, eh? Touch of the Mata Haris, even?"

"She is the daughter of Lord Farrier."

"Archie Farrier?" said Sir Roderick in a faint voice.

"So I understand."

"Can't believe it. Little Alice, I've known her since she was so high. Surely, some mistake."

"I'm afraid not."

Sir Roderick pondered. "Extraordinary thing. Poor old George making an ass of himself with some flapper at his age. Never felt the slightest inclination in that direction. Dorothy and I drew stumps years ago". Aware of Carruthers he collected himself. "How did Five discover all this?"

"Among other things, sir, they've been tapping the Home Secretary's telephone," said Carruthers with a touch of relish. There was traditionally no love lost between MI5 and MI6.

"Good God," said Sir Roderick, instinctively glancing at his own telephones. "Isn't that illegal?"

"More ill-advised, I would say." They looked at each other, surmising.

Finally, Sir Roderick remarked, "What ought we to do?"

"Refer it, sir, I think."

"You mean...?"

"Yes."

Sir Roderick saw choppy waters ahead. His thoughts travelled wistfully back to the long snow-covered horizons of Outer Mongolia, the squat grey houses of Ulan Bator, the oriental calm of a half-forgotten embassy. He wished he was elsewhere.

"This fellow Bond," he said as Carruthers began to leave, "has rather an exciting life, works quite hard, no one seems to bother about his affairs with women," adding, "being a secret agent, I mean."

"I wouldn't know, Sir Roderick."

Two hundred miles east of Moscow, inconveniently situated in a forest near Kovrov, the Citadel, a windowless concrete block now overgrown with ivy, housed the Codes and Cyphers Section. This Monday morning the usual Chekovian gloom had settled over the dozens of dark-suited figures at their identical pine desks. Large, stolid messengers came and went with sheaves of telexes. One man only appeared cheerful, chuckling from time to time; it was his duty to read the latest James Bond novel.

One of the gloomy figures looked up from his desk. "Dimitri Dimitrivitch, why do we really need details of the milk quota in Bechuanaland?"

"It is part of a larger pattern, Ivan Ivanovitch."

"What pattern?"

"That we shall never know."

"Must I decode it?"

"Yes, Ivan Ivanovitch, it is your job. You wish to have a job?"

"Of course. What else could I do?"

"Well, then Ivan Ivanovitch."

Another telex landed on his desk; he read it several times. "Bad news from London Station."

"How bad?"

"Very bad. Bulldog has reported that due to a sexual scandal in the British Cabinet the government will soon fall."

"That is very bad. You know how the Politburo dislikes change of any kind."

"Who can blame them? They wish to keep their jobs. They are old men."

"Shall we file it?"

"Yes, in the Gulag file." It was the nearest they allowed themselves a joke.

The man reading the Ian Fleming novel said admiringly, "This agent, Bond, he is too clever for us."

"Do not worry, Leon Leonovitch, he is most likely working on our side."

"How can we tell?"

"Well, to begin with, did he go to one of their public schools? The private ones, that is."

"Yes."

"Did he go to their Cambridge College?"

"Probably."

"Is he a member of one of their exclusive upper class clubs for men only."

"Yes."

"And is he unmarried?"

"Yes."

"Does he drink a lot?"

"Yes."

"Then, Leon Leonovitch, he is surely a double agent."

Chapter Six

Tim was at his desk, black coffee and Alka-Seltzer to hand. "May I?" said Simon, reaching for the familiar tubular bottle.

"Where were you last night?" said Tim.

"With you at least some of the time. We ended up in Esmeralda's Barn."

"With me?"

"No," said Simon, "I think we left you in the Grapes."

"I'm afraid," said Tim after a while, "that I've got a job for you."

"Not another dotty professor?"

"Not exactly. Ginger's going ahead with his documentary on Dylan. Apparently Sally, his production assistant, has gone sick, probably pregnant if I know anything about it. Can you help?"

"I reckon," said Simon.

"By the way," added Tim, "have you seen the *Express* today? Page two, pictures of your Wanda girl and the Home Secretary. Separate stories of course and different columns. They're on to something."

Simon studied the page. Wanda, glamorous and glittering, was shown emerging from the Arethusa Club on the arm of Nikki. The Home Secretary was shown meeting a deputation of Assistant Chief

Constables at the House of Commons. Very few of the millions of readers would see any significance in the juxtaposition of the pictures.

Simon found Ginger in his office, feet up, rebellious. "Hello, cock, come to join the sinking ship? I don't think the stupid pricks round here want me to do this documentary. It's too real for them, they spend time doing arse-creeping programmes about the bloody home Secretary."

"I know," said Simon.

"Well, fuck 'em, I say. I'm going to do this my way and if they don't like it..." He broke off to re-light a repulsive old pipe.

"How did you get it past Hilda?" said Simon impressed.

"I didn't exactly. I played another game and told Hopkins I was planning a documentary about that Welsh windbag, *George* Thomas. Portrait of a Parliamentarian or some such crap. I got a project number which means I can spend some cash. What do you know about Dylan?"

"Apart from drinking, you mean?"

"Don't you start," said Ginger crossly, "you'd think he never wrote a bloody poem the way some people go on. Anyway, we're going to do a recce and you can make some notes about where we've been."

"Rather like Tim," murmured Simon.

"What?"

"Nothing. When do we start?"

"Meet me in the lobby at twelve."

Breakfast in Chester Square. Lady Farrier looked up from her newspaper. "First of all it was an Arab and now it's a German."

Her husband, deep in the *Financial Times*, muttered, "Who was what, darling?"

"Alice. The *Express* has a photograph of Alice with a Mr.Nikki von something, who I presume is a German."

"Oh, *him*, he's an art crook. It's just Max making mischief as usual. He's getting at me."

"Don't you think you should let Alice know?"

"That girl's not stupid. Anyway she calls herself Wanda nowadays for some reason."

"Perhaps *I'd* better have a word with her," said Lady Farrier, picking up *The Times*. "You never know with the Germans, do you? I remember when I was a girl there was a divorce case in which some quite respectable man was accused of Hunnish Practices. We all wondered what they were."

"Quite so, darling."

Simon arrived in the lobby to find Kitty on duty, very much the furious little redhead. "You should be ashamed of yourself."

Taken aback Simon began, "I don't know…"

"You know perfectly well. What's more this is by no means the end of the matter. I'm taking it up with the management, I can tell you. Poor girl."

"I really…"

Fortunately at that moment Ginger bustled up, took in the scene and hurried Simon out into a waiting taxi.

"All men are pigs," was Kitty's parting shot.

In the taxi Simon said, "What the hell was all that about?"

"Christ, don't you know? Leo's put Wendy up the spout and as usual is trying to wriggle out of it."

A bit later Simon said, "Tim seems to think that Sally is in the club."

"He does, does he?" said Ginger quite affably. "Well, it's not me. At least I don't think so. I've barely laid a finger on her, in fact it's about all I have done as Leo would say. She's not really my type."

Simon changed the conversation. "Where are we going?"

"Paddington," said Ginger. "Dylan's starting point coming up from Swansea."

The taxi set them down at The Load of Hay by the entrance to the station. "We should really start with a nip of Bass and a ham sandwich in the buffet," said Ginger.

"Why?"

"That's what Dylan did on his first arrival in London in 1933." Ginger laughed. "And for Christ's sake don't get your finger stuck in a beer bottle."

"Why on earth would I do that?" asked Simon.

"Dylan did."

"How do you know?"

"Read *Adventures in the Skin Trade* sometime. Bizarre account of his first days in London. On one occasion," said Ginger as they entered the pub, "Dylan took two days to get from here to Soho."

After a pint he asked the landlord if he remembered the poet. "I probably knew him but then there's always been a lot of people called Thomas in here. Quite a few called Dylan. The Welsh seem to need a drink or two after the journey. Was he a tall man with a beard?"

"Not exactly."

"I tell you what," said the landlord moving towards a new customer, "Ask old Dick over there, he was once on a newspaper, he should know about poets."

Ginger and Simon carried their drinks over to where Dick was sitting with three other old men, all in dark suits with waistcoats; one had a mongrel dog half-asleep under the table. They readily accepted pints of beer after Dick had said he remembered Dylan. "Tall man with a beard," added Dick, "very fine poet."

"Did he ever talk about poetry?" asked Ginger.

"Not poetry," said another old man, "he talked a lot about whippets."

After they had accepted another round of drinks Ginger said, "Thanks, gentlemen, all very interesting, we've got to move on."

The old men nodded their thanks. "I don't reckon," said one old man pensively, "that he was a tall man with a beard."

"You never know," said Dick.

In the taxi Ginger said, "We'll just shoot the exterior. What we really want to know is where he stopped off on his way to Soho and who he was with."

"His wife?"

"Doubtful. Rocky sort of marriage. But, then, most are."

"Are you married?" said Simon.

"Was. Divorced last year. Polish girl, she pushed off home."

"To Poland?"

"To bloody Ealing."

"Sorry about that."

"I'm not," said Ginger.

"It's not easy to tell on the programme, is it?" said Simon.

"Tell what?"

"If anyone is married. I mean, I don't even know about Toby."

"Got a wife in the country somewhere and sees her at week-ends. Tim isn't but wants to marry Pippa when he's drunk. Who else?"

"Leo?"

"Hardly, old cock. No one would have him. Here we are."

The taxi had pulled up outside the 'French' in Dean Street. "Better hold on to this," said Ginger, "We've got lots of places to visit." He engaged in a brisk deal with the taxi driver. Entering the pub he was greeted warmly by several customers who quickly finished their drinks. Ginger bought a round and was soon deep in local gossip.

One of the customers, a young man wearing a very frayed Old Etonian tie asked Simon amiably enough to lend him a pound. Pleasantly relaxed by now Simon handed him a note and asked him what he did.

"How do you mean?"

"Do you work?"

"What at?"

"I mean, have you a job?" said Simon.

The young man still looked perplexed. "I'm expecting a cheque."

"Like Billy Bunter?"

"Exactly."

Ginger introduced another acquaintance who was carrying a bulging black brief case. "You must congratulate Torrin."

"Why?"

"He's just been declared a vexatious litigant by the High Court, haven't you?"

"I have indeed, I have indeed," said Torrin blandly.

"Whatever is that?" said Simon.

"Well..." began Torrin.

"Oh, God, not the whole boring story again," said Ginger, "just take it from me that the High Court knew what it was doing, he's very vexatious."

"I say…" began Torrin again.

"It's all right, old cock," said Ginger amiably, "we're on your side. Let's have another round." A short while later he glanced at his watch and said, "On bloody, on. We've got to keep on the Dylan trail. Who's coming to the 'Swiss'?" The acquaintances decided to stay where they were.

Carefree, Ginger and Simon strolled round the corner of Old Compton Street to the Swiss, followed by the taxi. After a couple of beers "to get the atmosphere" they boarded the taxi for the real hinterland of Soho pubs, that Bermuda triangle of Bohemians: the Fitzroy in Charlotte Street, the Wheatsheaf in Rathbone Place and the nearby Marquis of Granby, all redolent of long lost Dylan days. Here the poet was still fresh in the memory, particularly if the memory was refreshed by a drink or two. Anecdotes, some even possibly true, were rolled out.

"Why have you come to America, Mr Thomas?"

"In pursuit of my life-long quest of naked women in wet mackintoshes."

"I hope you are making notes," said Ginger as they emerged at closing time. Simon looked at his watch; it was ten past three; he felt he had been drinking all day. "Just think," continued Ginger once more in the taxi, "of the other recces we'll have to do. Chelsea for instance: the Queen's Elm, the Australian, the Crossed Keys, the Markham, the Anglesey and the King's Head and Eight Bells..."

Back in Soho in decaying Meard Street they descended the crumbling steps into the Mandrake Club, a vast subterranean cave of strange arches and alcoves reaching back into shadowy recesses. Half a dozen or so customers were standing at the bar; others were sitting at tables playing chess or occupying themselves more intimately in the alcoves.

Simon and Ginger were greeted by the frayed Etonian and the vexatious litigant for whom he bought yet another round of drinks; beer had now given way to whisky. "Expenses, old cock," said Ginger expansively, prompting the Etonian to borrow another pound from Simon.

The afternoon wore on. Simon had long passed feeling hungry and was now on that plateau of drunkenness when life appears agreeably remote and timeless. He even listened to the saga of litigation with uncomprehending sympathy. Ginger looked at his watch. "Four o'clock. To the Harlequin for the striptease."

The taxi took them to an alley off Trafalgar Square. "Did Dylan come here?"

"He would have done."

The club was a small room, smoky, crowded, noisy. Ginger ordered two light ales. "How much for the strip today?"

"Half-a-crown," said the barmaid grinning. "Money refunded if not satisfied."

They descended into a dimly-lit cellar where a dozen or so men were seated round the walls, chatting and drinking. A tall beautiful Jamaican young woman entered carrying a record which she placed on a wind-up gramophone. The chattering stopped. The Jamaican began to dance to the music slowly shedding her clothes until she was naked. General applause. She chatted briefly, dressed and went up the stairs carrying her record. Ginger introduced Simon to several drinkers. One called 'the Commander' and much more drunk than the rest said, "Good to meet you, faute de mieux actually," and relapsed into bemused silence.

Round about five-thirty when the pubs re-opened Ginger's homing instinct (as a former BBC radio producer) aroused a desire to visit the George, one of the legendary watering holes near Broadcasting House.

At various stages of the evening Simon encountered a famous poet, a very fat actor and someone wearing a cape and carrying a silver-topped cane, each happy to accept a drink. He had now more or less forgotten the reason for the recce believing it had something to do with the Home Secretary; he explained this laboriously to a bearded BBC features producer who nodded sympathetically.

Next day he barely remembered the taxi journey home ("I'm not taking him if he's going to be sick") the search for keys, the long, lurching climb up the stairs, finding the light switch, the toppling struggle to undress ... oblivion...

That evening, in contrast to Ginger's recce, Quentin and Pippa attended another of Kim Adrian's parties. Quentin went because of his insatiable thirst for gossip, Pippa because she was having second thoughts about Wanda's suggestion to join the Circuit. They arrived at Cavendish Mews at the same time as Wanda. "Darling," said Pippa, "isn't this a bit of a busman's holiday for you?"

"Don't know about busman," said Wanda cheerfully, "I remember a rather dishy taxi driver once..."

"No attachés?" asked Pippa.

"Day off, evening off or whatever. You were quite right about Roumania, very heavy. I've only dropped in to see Kim before going on hols with Nikki."

"No more George Worthington?" said Quentin.

"What a hoot," said Wanda leading the way into the mews house, "all that guff in the press, you'd think we were shagging. Three or four lunches and the odd reception. Not even a bottom nip. I asked him if he'd ever been unfaithful to Margaret and, poor dear, he looked genuinely surprised. You must say I did my best."

"Darling, you did."

As usual at the top of the stairs a suave, smiling Kim. "Didn't expect you," kissing Wanda, "but always welcome of course. Someone you know, by the way."

"Several, I would have thought," said Wanda moving into the party with Pippa. A familiar figure with his back to them. "Hi!" said Wanda. Lord Farrier turned, beaming, unsurprised.

"Might I suggest, my darling, that friend Kim dishes up a mildly better champagne?"

"I doubt if they notice the plonk," remarked Wanda glancing around.

"I don't think you've met Pippa."

"Delighted," said her father. "You have very beautiful eyes."

"Is that all?" said Pippa amused.

"No," giving her an appraising look, "definitely not all. May I get you a drink?"

"He's rather a poppet, isn't he?" said Wanda. "I think I see my aviator."

Later in Kim's study he said to Wanda, "Does he know."

"What?"

"That she works for Metro."

"Don't think so."

"Should he?"

"I don't see why."

"Do you mind?"

"Heavens, no, said Wanda. "Makes a change from South Kensington."

The party was over. The two "resting" actors collected glasses and ashtrays, replaced bottles in fridges and cupboards. Kim withdrew to his bedroom, a place of self-indulgent luxury, and lay down on his wide quilted bed to smoke a cigarette. After a while he changed into a crimson silk dressing-gown, admired himself in a full-length mirror and moved across to where a small portrait by John of a young curly haired boy hung on the wall. Carefully he removed the painting to reveal the cover of a spy hole. This he slid to one side and put his eye to the aperture. In a softly lit bedroom similar to his own two naked figures were caressing each other. "Anything that turns you on," murmured Pippa, "anything... except..." Her words were lost to Kim.

He pressed an adjacent bell-push. A minute or two later Jimmy, the younger of the actors entered the room wearing swimming trunks. Kim beckoned him to the spy hole and as he began observing Kim stroked his body, gently lowered his trunks, splayed his slim legs and moved up behind him.

Some time later as Kim was sitting in his study he heard the front door open and shut. Looking out of a window he saw Lord Farrier and Pippa getting into the Bentley that waited in the Mews. Returning to his desk he made a small entry in an account book.

The first touches of autumn, wet leaves on the pavements, smoky air, reflected Simon's mood as he reached the office by 10.30, for the morning meeting. Tim offered him the Alka-Seltzer bottle. and said "Leo, Pippa, stay," then to Muriel, "Get Toby down here. We must tidy up this bloody documentary."

"It's fine," said Leo defensively.

"So you say."

Toby bustled in carrying his clipboard. "Everything under control," he said, eyeing Leo. "All the filming's been done, I'm writing the commentary and we've just heard from the Private Office that Worthington will do the interview next Wednesday. What's the panic?"

"No panic," said Tim, picking up a newspaper. "I'm merely interested in how far this Wanda business is going. You lot began by using her to dig out something from his past and now the papers are suggesting they are having it off." He indicated a headline, *Home Secretary at Home?*'and read out,

"Rumours are circulating in Westminster that George Worthington is under pressure to deny charges about his private life. A spokesman from the Home Office said that it was no concern of the Home Office. The Home Secretary was not available for comment and Downing Street refused to comment apart from denouncing muckraking in the media."

"So what," said Leo. "Quite amusing."

"Amusing to my Aunt Fanny!" said Tim crossly. "Just as long as we don't feature in it. I've already had Hilda on asking what it's all about. She says it's disgraceful."

"The Home Sec?"

"Of course not. The bloody newspapers. She said we must ignore the whole thing."

Toby looked complacent. "I'll get him to deny everything in the interview and then we'll put out the profile as soon as possible. Bloody good publicity."

"What about your chum Wanda?" asked Tim.

"Off abroad any day," said Pippa. "She's not likely to say anything."

"And Kim Adrian?"

"Not in his interest, I fancy!" said Pippa.

"O.K," said Tim, picking up his backscratcher, "get cracking." Simon went out of the room with Pippa but she ignored him.

Some time later Ginger rolled into Tim's office looking remarkably unscathed by the previous day's excesses. "Help yourself," said Tim indicating the Alka-Seltzer.

"Don't need that cissy stuff," said Ginger parking himself in the armchair. "A couple of pints will set me right."

"How did the recce go?"

"Fine. Lots of Dylan's old pals still around. But I'll tell you one thing. We ended with a slight piss-up in the George and did you know that Hopkins has been having a bit on the side with one of the B.H. secretaries for years?"

"Interesting."

"It's more than interesting, matey. Next time he comes the high horse with me I'll say 'How's Susie these days'.   That should screw him."

"And your bloody future, said Tim. "You know what he'll do, go straight to Hilda and get you sacked. You're hardly her flavour of the month as it is. Think about it for once."

"Fuck 'em." said Ginger amiably.

"I reckon," said Tim looking at his watch, "I'll join you in a pint or two."

Hilda was standing in the club with a reluctant entourage. "Come here, both of you." Tim and Ginger joined her group. "First about the Home Secretary. I saw the chairman this morning and he's particularly concerned about these ridiculous rumours of a scandal. He wouldn't elaborate, but I was able to assure him that we were not likely to include rumours in your documentary. Too many biographies these days dig into the more sensational side of their subjects. Quite unnecessary. I remember Lord Beaverbrook once telling me that certain people tried to spread rumours about his private life, all untrue of course. After all, as he reminded me, he was a son of the Manse. We know that George Worthington could not be involved in anything like that."

She glared at her entourage.

"There have been Cabinet Ministers…" began Tim.

"Very regrettably," said Hilda sharply. "If you must refer to that vile man Lloyd George. I'm told none of the secretaries at Number Ten were safe, even in the Cabinet Room, when he was PM. Thank goodness times have changed."

"He did win the war," murmured Tim.

"Trust you to try and defend him. My point is that he took advantage of his position to harass young girls who were working for him." Hilda waved her glass. "It's as though H-P and Toby and *you* for that matter were over-familiar with your secretaries. One thing at least I was able to reassure the chairman that there was no such hanky-panky among the staff at Metro."

Ginger choked slightly over his beer. "As for you, Ruddle, I've had the Welsh Office on the phone wanting to know if they can help with your documentary. Well, of course I sent them about their business. I won't have Whitehall poking their noses into our programmes. It's a very good idea to do a little film about the working life of an MP, particularly the ethnic kind, they often get overlooked at Westminster. George Thomas is a nice choice, might get somewhere one day, not quite the Cabinet I fancy."

Fortunately for Ginger at that moment Hilda spotted the editor of Forum. "Come here, Andrew. I'm told that last night you caused my good friend the Cardinal Archbishop of Westminster grave embarrassment when he came in to appear on the programme."

Well…" began Andrew.

"Don't argue. I haven't time to discuss it now but I expect a full explanation after lunch." She departed.

"What was all that about?" asked Ginger.

"Not my fault," said Andrew. "The Cardinal was in hospitality after changing as usual into his full purple. He decided to have a nervous pee before the prog and trundled off down the corridor but apparently got lost on the way back and ended up at Reception. Dear little Wendy of course directed him to the drama studio where they were recording 'The Three Musketeers'. I had to rescue him."

Passing Reception later on Ginger grinned at Wendy. "Didn't know you had the hots for priests."

Wendy bridled. "How the hell did I know that he was a real Cardinal?"

"Well," said Ginger, "did he make a pass at you?"

"Of course not."

"Then you should have realised that he was not an actor."

"You are silly," said Wendy.

Chapter Seven

Maunsel Street is a quiet thoroughfare between the traffic of Horseferry Road and the calm of Vincent Square. The junior member of MI5 approached the "safe house" from Victoria. In the autumn evening sunshine boys of Westminster School were kicking a ball about on the Square and he recalled that Somerset Maugham as a young medical student had lodged here - very early shades of Ashenden.

It is a street of thirty or so similar late Georgian houses; there were several parked cars, no vans or motor cycles, nothing unusual. He took in the scene with eyes trained to observe. He slipped the key easily in the Chubb lock. Several desperate thrusts failed to move the front door. He remembered the mortise. A middle-aged woman letting herself into the house opposite eyed him curiously. What was meant to be a routine entry had become an incident.

Stumbling slightly into the shadowy living-room he hurriedly drew the curtains of the window facing the street and switched on the lights. In spy novels secret agents suspected they were being followed to safe houses, peering through curtains in quickly darkened rooms, checking shadows. He doubted if anyone had followed him.

The living-room was well furnished, books on the shelves, pictures on the walls, radio and television, a desk with a reading lamp, a drinks cupboard, ashtrays. He poured himself a small whisky and sat down in one of the chintz-covered armchairs. Looking round he wondered what kind of person bought and furnished safe houses. Did they pose as genuine owners ("Need a base in town, old boy.") talk about surveys, supervise removal vans, hire cleaners, speak to the milkman and postman, chat to the neighbours? Noticing a stain on the carpet he wondered who had used this particular house: witnesses, defectors, double agents, 'grasses'. Couldn't he have met his contact at a railway station or in a supermarket? He supposed not; this was the secret world.

'Secret from whom?' he had once asked when he joined the department. Nothing is surely secret per se. If in doubt, they said, classify everything: Most Secret, Secret, Confidential, Restricted, take your pick, and once classified it remains so indefinitely.

Ten minutes later the doorbell rang three times and he hurriedly admitted Carruthers, trim and self-assured in dark suit and bowler hat. He greeted the junior member affably despite their disparate ranks because this was MI5 property with no official link to MI6.

Declining a drink Carruthers glanced out into the small paved garden. He knew MI5 would have bugged the house, very probably also MI6, Special Branch and almost certainly the Soviet Embassy.

"The garden, I think, don't you?"

The junior member, who had not considered the likelihood of bugging, looked momentarily surprised. "Yes, of course."

"Put me in the picture," said Carruthers who had been a soldier during the war. One member of the department who had been in the R.A.F. went round saying, "What's the latest gen?" The junior member who hoped that his co-operation would land himself a job with MI6 brought him up-to-date on Worthington. They moved on to MI5 and Special Branch surveillance of Soviet Embassy officials and radio intercepts of London-Moscow traffic. He also handed over some minutes of recent meetings.

"My director is still interested in Philby."

"Waste of time," said Carruthers, "since he was cleared by the Foreign Secretary. He's doing a small job for us in Beirut."

To lighten the conversation the junior member said, "Good joke the other day."

"What was that?" said Carruthers.

"Anonymous denunciation of Anthony Blunt." Carruthers choked violently.

"Are you all right, sir?"

"Of course," said Carruthers recovering himself. "Good joke."

The light was fading and they went indoors. The junior member again offered Carruthers a whisky. At that moment the telephone rang.

"Are you expecting a call?" said Carruthers suspiciously.

"No."

"Well you'd better answer it."

The junior member gingerly picked up the phone. "Hello..." He listened for a short while. "No, I'm afraid not." He replaced the receiver.

"Who was it?"

"Someone who wanted the Army and Navy stores."

Carruthers put on his overcoat and bowler hat. "Any further information, we would be most grateful. What contact will you use in future?"

"Clarence Rules," said the junior member feeling truly conspiratorial; the code was named after a pub in Whitehall used by the security services. "A chalk mark on Nelson's column."

"Quite so."

There was a loud knock at the front door.

"Whatever next?" said Carruthers irritably. "You'll have to answer that."

The junior member peered round the door revealing a young postman with a parcel. "Can't get anyone next door. I wondered if you wouldn't mind taking this in."

"I suppose so..."

"Sign here, please. Thanks, guvnor."

"Are you sure this is a *safe* house?" asked Carruthers glancing at his watch. He had a meeting with his Soviet controller at nine on Hampstead Heath, not his favourite rendezvous because of the sexual marauders. His controller, who had a black sense of humour thought it was ideal cover.

The morning meeting in the editor's office of the great newspaper. "Anything more on Worthington?"

"I think we've pushed it as far as we can go."

"Kim Adrian says it's all a bit of a lark," said the Diary editor.

"We know that," said the editor, "but the Old Man wants us to chase up Farrier. Nailing his daughter as a hooker is one way. Worthington makes it a good story. I think it's about time someone asked a question in the House. Can you fix that?"

"Surely."

When Simon arrived in the office next day he found Toby already hard at work on the typewriter, Melanie busy on the telephone. "Must get cracking", said Toby "the Private Office has just rung to say they want to bring forward the Home Sec. interview to this Friday."

"What can I do?"

"Check quotes and dates when I've done the intro and questions." Toby smiled bleakly. "Don't want another Baggins affair, do we?" Melanie frowned. Observing them together Simon found it hard to reconcile Toby, self-absorbed, polite, unemotional and Melanie, shy, modest, fragile, with the stark lust of that Saturday morning.

"You might tell Pippa, will you, of the new arrangements," said Toby, "she's going to direct. Thank God we've got Fred Pope as cameraman. Don't want any histrionics, we're shooting it in the Home Office."

Simon found Pippa in the canteen having coffee with Ginger. "Hello, cock," said Ginger. "Feel like another recce?"

"I do not."

"Please yourself. By the way, have you put in your exes yet?"

"No, not yet, I wasn't sure…'

"Better let me do it, cock. We don't want a balls-up, that bastard Hopkins queries everything. He really is…"

"Not again, Ginger dear," said Pippa. "What with you and Toby it's a wonder that Metro shows a profit." Before Ginger could protest she went on, "Simon, darling, we were thinking of having a jolly supper this evening, Ginger, Sally, me and you. How about it?"

"Fine."

"On exes," said Ginger.

"But of course."

Old Benno was on the programme that evening. A bishop had written a book denying the existence of God and it was only right that Benno in the newly-assumed role of the Almighty's P.R.O. on earth should present his views on the matter. As usual Toby refereed the contest. And as usual, each side stuck stubbornly to his own set of opinions and neither answered a straight question. In the lift afterwards Toby just managed to head off Ziggy from trying to sell French letters to the bishop. Old Benno was greatly amused.

In hospitality Hilda swayed towards the bishop. "Call yourself a Christian," she barked at the startled cleric. "You're a disgrace to the cloth. I remember before the war meeting the Dean of Canterbury, the

Red Dean we called him. He stood up for Stalin of all people. I said the same to him."

"But, Hilda, dear, said Benno coming to the rescue of the bishop, "Hewlett-Johnson, poor man, was a deluded Marxist."

"Deluded fiddlesticks. He was an atheist. How dare he preach in the cathedral?" The bishop managed to edge away leaving Hilda and Benno to continue arguing.

Later Benno joined Tim, Toby and Pippa. "I see that your tease with poor old George Worthington has worked rather well."

"Our tease?" said Toby. "Your tease more likely. You put us on to Kim Adrian."

"So I did, so I did," said Benno, letting his hand brush Pippa's thigh. "All politicians need teasing constantly. Only the ones with a sense of humour, the very few, don't mind. I was hearing only the other day that the Foreign Secretary…"

Hilda joined them.

"Has that whisky priest departed? I saw him filling up his glass. Thank heaven for you, Benno, although there were times in the past when I seem to remember that even you were tempted by drink ... and women." She laughed indulgently.

"Dead sea fruit, my dear Hilda, as I was just telling these charming young people," said Benno moving his hand away from Pippa. "Talking of which I hear that you are doing a programme about Dylan Thomas."

"I don't know where you heard that, Benno. It was a typically irresponsible idea of Ruddle's and I said

Benno

no firmly. As I told him we are not here to glorify drunken poets. Not that I disapprove of them having the odd drink. John Betjeman once told me that he and his friend Evelyn Waugh used to enjoy the very occasional glass of wine."

"At least you wouldn't have to interview him," said Benno. "I once did a live interview with poor old Brendan and the only brief I got from the producer was that if he said a four-letter word I wasn't to laugh. In the event he was totally drunk and merely sang a little song."

"Disgraceful," said Hilda. "But we are, as you know, doing a profile of the Home Secretary, a fine stamp of man. What's more it should put paid to these silly rumours in the gutter press. There's far too much about people's sex lives in the papers these days. I blame that disgusting Lady Chatterley book. It was the present Home Secretary who tried hard to suppress it and look what happened. As Mr Griffiths-Jones said at the recent trial, 'Is it a book that you would ever wish your wife or your servants to read?'"

"By the way," turning to Tim, "I'm glad to see the chairman's daughter in the papers these days, it should help her modelling career. Charming girl, we could do with more like her at Metro, don't you think, Pippa?"

"Surely."

Later that evening Ginger suggested that they went to Nick's Bistro.

"Oh, God, it's a bear-garden, said Pippa. "Can't we go to the Meridiano and at least eat in comfort?"

"With all those toffee-nosed twits…" began Ginger.

"He's off again on his class thing," said Sally. "We'll get his bit about bread and dripping next."

She was a pert, bubble-cut blonde and Simon had recently become friendly with her.

"O.K. duckie," said Ginger.

"Providing you try and behave," said Pippa.

"Such as?"

"No farting, for Christ's sake."

"I'll try," said Ginger.

The Meridiano was almost opposite the San Frediano in the Fulham Road and similar in decor and style. They were shown to a well-spaced table on the upper floor. Pippa greeted one or two other customers and Ginger muttered about "bloody snobs". As the evening wore on and, mainly at Ginger's insistence, more bottles of wine were ordered Simon became hazily aware that Sally not Pippa was to be his likely partner.

Most of the conversation was gossip about Metro. Simon learnt that almost all producers and presenters were screwing some other members of the staff. When he finally mentioned Toby and Melanie it evoked no surprise. "Randy little runt," said Ginger. "His secretaries usually last about three months. The last threatened to tell his wife."

"What about Muriel?"

"Long, long affair with one of the film editors."

"And Quentin?"

"No live-in boy friend, I believe," said Pippa. Plays the field, young actors, male models."

Simon rotated his wine glass.

"Isn't there anyone ... Hilda for instance?"

"The story goes," said Ginger, "that when her father worked at the Treasury he took her across one day to Number Ten and Lloyd George offered to show her the Cabinet Room. That's why she blows up whenever the old goat is mentioned."

"How on earth do you know that?" said Simon.

"Tim told me."

"How did he know?"

"From old Benno. Hilda confided in him one evening."

"How about old Ziggy?" said Sally.

"Not so old, duckie," said Ginger. "More than once he's apparently stopped the lift between floors with one of the girls from the post-room."

"At least he's not likely to get her pregnant," said Pippa and they all laughed rather loudly.

Ginger beckoned the wine waiter. "No more, for Christ's sake," said Pippa. "I've had enough of Tim passing out on me. You remember, Simon?"

" I do."

"Can't hold it," said Ginger. "O.K. let's go back to my place for a night cap."

"Whatever that is," said Sally looking round for her handbag. Ginger was studying the bill. "Here, is this fucking thing correct?"

"How much?"

"Thirty-seven quid."

"Lot of wine, you know."

"I can't put any more on the Thomas project number, they'll have my balls off."

"Don't worry, old dear," said Pippa, "We'll let the Home bloody Secretary pay, won't we, Simon?"

"O.K. by me."

On the way out they spotted Wanda dining with Nikki. "We're a bit pissed," said Pippa.

"A lot pissed if you ask me."

"See you soon."

"No, darling, remember we're off to the Caribbean."

"Give my love to the darkies," said Ginger.

In the Fulham Road Simon shouted "taxi" at a passing car.

"Don't need one," said Ginger. "Only live round the corner."

They walked unsteadily along Walton Street, turning into Hasker Street's row of tiny houses. Sally held on to Simon's arm. Ginger sang a few verses of "Little Angeline". On the steps of his house he fumbled for his keys, blaspheming vigorously. Once inside both women made for the bathroom. Ginger poured himself and Simon a whisky. "You take the upstairs bedroom, old cock. I'm in here. Good luck. By the by," said Ginger winking theatrically, "she likes it up the bum."

"I heard that," said Pippa coming down the stairs. "You really are a disgusting man."

"Hope so," said Ginger leading the way into the bedroom.

Chapter Eight

"I want you all in my office immediately." Tim held the telephone away from his ear until Hilda had ceased barking.

"I…"

"Don't argue. I expect you in five minutes."

Tim looked across at Muriel. "Crisis, God knows why. She wants the entire Home Sec. team."

An angry Toby followed by Pippa and Simon assembled in Tim's office. "What the hell…?"

"I know less than you, dear boy," said Tim. "Where's Leo?"

"God knows."

"O.K. we'd better get going."

Hilda drunk could be confusing; Hilda sober first thing in the morning could be terrifying. "I don't know what any of you have done. All that I can say is that something has happened and I mean to find out what."

"What exactly are we talking about?" said Tim gently.

"You undoubtedly know more about it than I do," said Hilda furiously. "I have just been with the chairman and I find that he wants to cancel the Home Secretary programme."

"Why?" said Toby bluntly.

"He's read these ridiculous rumours in the press about George Worthington being involved in some kind of scandal and he says that it makes us look as though we were somehow responsible. I assured him that was most unlikely but nevertheless he wants to see you all. " She glared at Tim. "What have you been up to?"

"Nothing, Hilda."

"Eleven o'clock then," said Hilda dismissing them, "in his office."

Out in the corridor Tim said, "I've only met the old boy once at some anniversary do."

"He's all right," said Toby. "But I must say it's a bit odd. Surely he can't believe this stuff about his daughter."

"Let's have coffee," said Pippa. "I think this may be interesting."

"Lord Farrier will see you now," said the elegant young secretary.

"Toby Gage, my dear fellow, do come in." The chairman walked towards them as they entered. Suddenly catching sight of Pippa he paused, collected himself, said "Please" beckoning them to several deep armchairs. The elegant secretary carried in a silver tray with equally elegant coffee pot and cups. Lord Farrier, once more the relaxed, suave tycoon smiled at Pippa.

"You are new here?"

"Not really, two years on Good Evening." She smiled back, no hint of complicity.

"I thought," said Lord Farrier, "that I would like to hear how you are getting on with the programme about my good friend George Worthington. As you are probably aware I am not concerned with the day to day running of Metro but, believe me, I watch with great interest and of course am particularly proud of Good Evening."

Tim looked puzzled. "We rather gathered from Hilda…"

"Ah, yes, I think perhaps Hilda occasionally gets the wrong end of the stick," he avoided Pippa's eyes, "and maybe she mistook my, er, concern for criticism. Now, Toby and all of you, brief me, as it were, about your progress..."

On the way down in the lift Toby said, "Very rum."

"I told you it would be interesting," said Pippa. Tim looked at her quizzically. Back in Toby's office they returned to the work of preparing for the interview. The phone rang and Melanie said, "Someone for you, Pippa."

"Hello, Miss Crowne," the voice was unfamiliar, "this is Lord Farrier's secretary. Would you like to come up here?"

"Certainly," said Pippa, then, "I'm just nipping out for a minute or two."

Lord Farrier had a flat as well as an office on the top floor of Metro Studios. Pippa was shown into a sumptuous drawing-room, shadowed now by venetian blinds. Farrier embraced her. "Shock of my life, darling. Why didn't you tell me?"

"Thought it might put you off, Archie."

"Good God, no, I wanted you the moment I met you at Kim's. How right I was, wasn't I?"

"You were."

"I want you now."

"Isn't this a bit tricky?" said Pippa.

"You mean Yvonne? She stands guard in my office, very loyal." He poured out some champagne.

Later, finishing the champagne together he asked, "How well do you know my daughter?"

"Great chums."

"How amusing. What's all this nonsense about her and George?"

"Just nonsense."

"Good. That was the only reason I thought of cancelling the programme. Didn't want to involve Alice or whatever she calls herself. I think Max is gunning for me in the *Express*." They chatted until Pippa glanced at her watch and said, "Reminds me, I'm on your payroll. They'll be wondering where I am."

"And where were you?"

"At the chairman's disposal?"

"Exactly."

"Will I see you tomorrow evening?"

"Surely."

On his way home from MI6 Sir Roderick called in at Pratt's. Going down the stairs he encountered the Prime Minister.

"How are you, Roddy? Haven't been to see me recently. Nothing up is there?"

"Well, as a matter of fact, Eddie, I wouldn't mind a word."

"Good fellow. How about lunch at Buck's sometime?"

"Bit more private, I fancy. Trifle urgent."

The Prime Minister looked benevolently at Roderick.

"Been working, eh? Better drop round to Number Ten. Not lunchtime, I've got some American chap about the bomb or something. Make it teatime. Old Mrs Henniker still does those scones you like."

"Delighted, Eddie."

"Not at all."

Strolling through Trafalgar Square at lunchtime Carruthers glanced at Nelson's column. Clear to his eyes if to no one else's were two chalk marks. That evening leaving the office he caught a 24 bus to Camden Town, changed to the Northern Line and got off two stations later at Belsize Park. It was all very inconvenient but "Clarence Rules" required such deception in an emergency. Avoiding the ancient lifts he lingered on the platform until the other passengers had left and then made for the staircase. It was gloomy, dirty and smelly; he mounted the circular stairs with increasing breathlessness. Halfway up he was thankful to meet the junior member of MI5.

"Out of training, young man, ' said Carruthers taking several deep breaths.

"Sorry about this, sir, the safe house was already booked."

They were back on formal terms away from Maunsel Street.

"I trust that it is important."

"Indeed. I thought you should know that the information about the Home Secretary has been found to be unsafe."

Carruthers was appalled. "How unsafe?"

"Totally."

"How do we know?"

"Our man in Metro," said the junior member, "discovered that it was all made up to publicise a programme they were making about George Worthington."

"I thought you said that they bugged his telephone."

"They did. The trouble was that they didn't read the calls accurately; they merely used them to confirm other information."

"And where did that originate?"

The junior member looked embarrassed. "I think it all started with the magazine *Private Eye*."

"Good God," said Carruthers.

Disaster loomed for him on two fronts. Not only had he briefed the Director for his visit to Downing Street but he had also assured his Soviet controller that a government scandal was imminent. "You were right, my boy, to let me know. Damn these stairs." He set off down to the platform. The junior member gloomily climbed back up to the street.

Hilda's monthly programme review meeting began with her in a surprisingly good mood. Viewing figures were up, Metro shares were buoyant and there had been no complaints to the I.T.A. It was too good to last. A Light Entertainment producer foolishly compared Good Evening with two of his own department's recent successes, The Knackers, a sitcom set in a slaughterhouse and The Strippers, a jokey serial about asset-stripping in the City.

Hilda exploded and the wretched producer was expelled from the meeting. Regaining her composure she announced, "You'll be glad to hear that the chairman is taking a personal interest in our important documentary about the Home Secretary." She glared at Tim. "I trust you will all ignore certain ridiculous rumours in the papers. And while we are on the subject of politics you will be interested to hear that I have decided to start a new political programme devoted to one subject only - whatever is the topic of the week. An in-depth study. Far too often," she glared at Andrew, "we gloss over the really vital issues of the day."

"Who will do it?" asked Tim.

"I have Toby in mind. After all, he respects politicians."

Tim caught Andrew's eye.

"And the producer?"

"You can spare Leo, can't you?"

"Certainly can. Have you got a title?"

"I have indeed," said Hilda pleased with herself. "It will be called Penetration."

Silence. Tim and Andrew avoided each other's eyes. "Do you think… " began Tim.

"Don't argue. You always manage to find fault with good ideas. I'm sure that many M.P.s will be eager to take part in Penetration."

"And quite a few ministers, I reckon," said Andrew.

"Quite so. Well, that's settled," said Hilda looking at her watch. "Back to work."

After she had left the room Andrew said, "Who's going to tell her?"

"You mean *how* is anyone going to tell her," said Tim.

"Not me."

"No, it's up to Leo."

"Should be good for a laugh."

"Poetic justice," said Tim.

Simon made his way to the club, happier nowadays in the company of Sally since the night of the supper party. Not only physically but also temperamentally she was a complete and restful contrast to Pippa. There was no unpredictable switch of moods and sex was no longer an instant and mechanical gratification. All in all Simon welcomed the change of partners and Pippa barely appeared to notice now that she had bigger fish to fry.

The previous evening in bed with Sally he had discussed his future on Good Evening, something he had never been able to do with Pippa since the only topics which interested her were herself and sex. His three-month contract had only two more weeks to run and neither Tim nor the management had suggested an extension. "Have you discussed it with him?" asked Sally.

"Not really."

"You must, angel. Tim's a nice guy and we all like him but he's not good on the hiring and firing business. He just lets things wander on until the dreaded Hopkins suddenly gives you the chop." She turned towards him. "Depends of course if you actually want to stay on the programme."

"What do you think?"

"About Good Evening?" asked Sally.

"Yes."

"Tricky. It's been going for over six years and I reckon that it's running out of steam. Nobody's fault, just the life of a daily programme like ours, over-exposure probably. Viewing figures are falling since the BBC started to compete with sitcoms against us."

"What's Tim think?"

"I reckon he knows, judging by the amount he drinks these days."

"Surely Hilda wants it to go on?" said Simon.

"Possibly, but she's nearing retirement, I fancy. It's not just the drink, she's losing grip."

"What about the presenters, H-P and co?"

"Oh, they'll be all right, just shift to another programme or the bloody BBC or something," said Sally.

Simon paused. "How about Ginger?"

"Don't worry about him," said Sally, "he's a survivor, the old sod."

"Do you like him?"

"You mean, did I like screwing him? He was O.K, a bit crude I suppose, but he'd been around and a girl likes a chap who knows what to do."

"I suppose I…" began Simon.

"No, sweetie, I'm not getting at you. In fact you're a bit of a relief after Ginger. A girl can have too much of a good thing." Sally looked quizzically at Simon.

"But you're all the same, you know."

"The same as what?" said Simon puzzled.

"Dear old Ginger with his blue collar affectations doesn't fool anyone."

"What *are* you talking about?"

"You're just a type," said Sally gently, "you, Tim and Ginger, English public school, emotionally retarded."

"We're what?" said Simon still puzzled.

"Darling, you can't help it but you all treat women as though they were slightly unwell men. You hold open doors, fetch drinks, light cigarettes, give them an arm and so on. But emotionally you can't cope, you feel much safer in your clubs, pubs, regiments, common rooms. Poor darlings we terrify you when we don't bore you."

"Well, stone the crows," said Simon amiably, "what brought this on?"

"Nothing brought it on, sweetie. The mere fact that you ask is really what I'm talking about. Never mind, we girls are supposed to be getting liberated, whatever that means, in these swinging Sixties."

"From what you've just said, isn't it about time we emotionally retarded chaps got ourselves liberated?"

"Brilliant idea. How about starting now?" said Sally.

Chapter Nine

The Prime Minister was in the Cabinet room reading *Phineas Finn* when the Home Secretary was shown in. "My dear George, forgive this but it's always a bit quieter in here. Whisky?"

"No thanks, Prime Minister."

The solitary portrait of Robert Walpole looked down with remote disdain. The Prime Minister tapped his copy of *Phineas Finn*, "I've always gone along with the view, haven't you, that if you notice what a chap is reading it'll tell you most things about him. For instance, Roddy was in here yesterday and he told me he was reading this James Bond fellow. Well, you might say, it's to do with his job but he said he actually enjoyed it. We all used to read Buchan, of course, but that was when we were young."

"I'm reading Walter Scott at the moment."

"Are you?"

There was a silence.

"To get back to Roddy," said the P.M. "you know how I dislike gossip, one of the bugbears of the Commons, people with nothing to do standing round gossiping. Last thing I want, you know, is to pry into ministers' private lives. But it seems, George, that some silly rumours are going round about you and Archie Farrier's daughter who is, and I find this hard to believe, no better than she ought to be.

Roddy says she knocks around with undesirables and so on. Well, we all remember before the war there was a bit of that going on, loose women, rather a fast set. But this time there's a political thing about it all, possible Russian involvement or something. You see the problem?"

"Yes, Prime Minister. I've known Alice for many years, a friend of the family."

"My dear fellow, I appreciate that."

"There have been some silly things in the Press. Surely you don't believe them?"

"Good Heavens, no. Long since I believed a word in the Press about anything. I remember Max saying that he owned his newspapers merely for propaganda, Empire Free Trade, that kind of rubbish. And *The Times* was completely unreliable, all that support Geoffrey gave to Neville over Hitler..."

"What exactly is being said? That I'm having an affair with this young woman?"

"I'm afraid so, George."

"I see."

"Far be it from me to moralise. I leave that to the bishops. We all take our pleasures where we may. I for one am quite happy with my Trollope."

"Your trollop, Prime Minister?"

The Prime Minister tapped his book. "Very relaxing, particularly the political ones."

"Yes, of course. I understand."

"I thought so, my dear fellow. Quite straightforward. What I suggest is for you to make a brief statement in the House. Best for you, best for the party."

There was a very long pause. George looked up at Walpole. The longest-serving Prime Minister whose hardworking brilliance and adroit management gave England prosperity at home and peace abroad, the shrewd First Lord of the Treasury whose mastery of detail enabled him to reform the nation's finances, the loyal servant of the Crown, generous friend, connoisseur of paintings, looked quizzical... this was the parliamentarian known in his day as "The Great Corrupter" who remarked "Every man has his price"; the politician who made a personal fortune out of politics; the spendthrift who lived more extravagantly than the richest dukes; the nepotist who loaded offices on his brothers and children; the toper whose wine merchant in one year collected over 500 dozen empties; a glutton who ordered one hundred pounds weight of chocolate at a time; the adulterer who built his mistress, Molly Skerret, a costly villa in Richmond Park ... How could George, honest, scrupulous, trustworthy, abstemious, faithful, dull George, compete with this exemplar of the full life? Wasn't there time for just one mould-breaking, adventurous decision?

"No, Prime Minister."
"No?"
"I'm afraid that it is all completely true."
"That you did have an affair with Archie's girl?"
"Yes, Prime Minister."

Another long pause. Robert Walpole's expression seemed to have changed to mild admiration and envy. The Prime Minister gazed thoughtfully down the long, empty, coffin-shaped Cabinet table. "I must say myself I've always thought young Alice - never heard this Wanda thing - a charming girl. Sorry to hear she's turned out to be a wrong 'un. Sorry for Archie as well. But I'm afraid it won't do, George, it won't do at all."

"I know."

"Afraid you'll have to go."

"Yes. I'm sorry to have caused you all this trouble."

The Prime Minister looked across the table. "My dear fellow, it's just a little local difficulty. Believe me, it'll all blow over in a few days. I've been in the game long enough to know that politicians have very short memories or they wouldn't be in politics. Just imagine if they had to recall what they said some while ago. Wouldn't do at all. The secret of the game in politics, my dear George, is to keep one step ahead of the other fellow, sometimes the Opposition, usually the Press. You've let me know the facts before they get out and we are both in a position to control events." He paused ruminatively. "Worse thing about this job, you know, is events." Then glancing down at his book, "That's about it, I fancy. Usual exchange of letters, you know the thing. The Press of course will print a few wild stories, that's their job. The Opposition will ask a few awkward questions, that's their job.

But it'll soon blow over. Anyway, good luck, my dear fellow."

George Worthington shook hands and, strangely elated, left the Cabinet room. The Prime Minister pressed a bell and a private secretary glided into the room. "Charles, tell Giles, will you, that he's to call me. Cabinet move." Alone once more in the peaceful, elegant room the Prime Minister continued his reading.

The first news of the Home Secretary's resignation was, as it happened, the one and only real scoop for a reporter from a local paper in Westmoreland who was standing in Downing Street with his wife and children as part of a tour round London on their first ever visit. He failed to spot it. The historic front door opened, out came a rather bewildered George Worthington, saw a group of people clustered nearby, said as firmly as he could, "I have resigned," got into his Humber and was driven away.

"Who was that, do you think?"

"I've seen the face before."

"What did he say?"

"Resigned or something, I think."

"I wonder why."

The tour guide, an Oxford undergraduate on vacation and impatient to get to a pub, said with total disregard for the facts, "On our left we have the noble portals of the Admiralty."

Tim was drinking a cup of tea and discussing that evening's running order with Leo when the ITN news-flash occurred. "What shall we do?" asked Leo. With barely a pause Tim said, "Scrub everything and go for the Home Sec. Christ knows we must have all the clips and info ready for your bloody documentary. Muriel, darling, get everyone in. Then to Leo, "A blow-up of Worthington for the studio. Likely running order, a good opening teaser, links to Westminster for live ITN insert and interviews with M.P's and studio discussions of course. Get cracking."

"Right," said Leo.

Toby, Pippa, Simon and a few others arrived chattering, astounded.

"Calm down, comrades," said Tim sharply, at his best as usual in a crisis. "Christ knows why he's done this, it doesn't bloody matter, we've got the opportunity to make a good programme out of the profile stuff. News will do their best at six o'clock but we can do better, a bloody sight better."

He looked down at his notes.

"Toby, start chatting up some M.P's, liaise with the ITN chaps down there. Leo, book a couple of political pundits, Perry, Paul, Tony... and a historian or someone to cover past sex scandals."

As they hurried out of the room he turned to Pippa. "How about Wanda, will she deny the whole thing, can we get her?"

"Doubt it, Tim, she went abroad yesterday, the Caribbean or somewhere."

Well get a good clip, something sexy for Christ's sake."

"Right." She paused at the door, "What about the chairman and Hilda?"

"Hard bloody luck," said Tim, "I'm not hanging around for their opinions. Anyway I believe Hilda's away for the day at some conference giving stick to Mrs Whitehouse and the Clean-Up-TV brigade."

"I thought Hilda wants to clean up TV," said Pippa.

"She does," said Tim, "but she reckons it's her job and not nosey-parkers like Mrs W and Pilkington. Now, back to business. Simon, book Old Benno. He can do the hypocrisy in high places stuff, public and private lives morality, public need to know, all that."

Toby reappeared. "How about the security angle?"

"Tricky. Have a word with the shadow Home Secretary, you know him don't you?" said Tim.

"Yes. Do you want me to dub the biog?" said Toby.

"If you've got time. H-P will do a long intro if we can't stop him. He'd also better do Benno in case the old villain gets too far into gossip."

"How about Fleet Street?"

"They'll all be bashing out their stories but try and get hold of one of the lobby boys."

Tim drank what remained of his tea. "Doubt if his family or friends will want to say much but someone can try his constituency association chairman and a few of the local yokels in Somerset or wherever. That's about it for the moment. Keep me informed."

The office emptied and Tim relaxed in his chair. The door slowly opened and Hammy wandered in, tousled and vague. "What's all the rush about?"

"Where the hell have you been?" said Tim.

"In the cutting room."

"Doing what?"

"A commentary for that elephant compilation."

Tim loaded his popgun. "Hammy, for Christ's sake, we dropped that bloody item two days ago."

"No one told me. Did you know that there was all that difference between Indian and African elephants and…"

"Buzz off, dear boy," said Tim "and help Toby with his commentary on the Home Secretary."

"A pity about the elephants," murmured Hammy leaving the office. "Which secretary...?"

A few minutes later H-P strode in, bristling with eagerness and authority. "Just heard the news. Bit of a bombshell, I must admit. Last man in my book to go off the rails. I suppose we're going to mention it?"

"It's the entire programme," said Tim calmly.

"Good heavens, is that wise?" said H-P taking a chair and looking stern.

"Don't know about wise but it's certainly news and you might say, current affairs."

H-P frowned. "A joke in slightly bad taste, Tim. After all we have the chairman's daughter to think of. What has Hilda said?"

"She's not back yet from that conference."

"Well in my opinion I think we must treat the whole subject with…"

The door burst open and Ginger entered. "Hey, how about old Worthy dipping his wick with luscious Wanda… Hello, H-P."

"Just what I meant, Tim," said H-P ignoring Ginger. "If we aren't careful we'll be competing with the gutter press."

"Bugger off, Ginger," said Tim, "and give Toby and Pippa a hand with the programme."

"Give her hand any day," said Ginger belching cheerfully as he left the office.

"Impossible man," said H-P with what he hoped was lofty dismissal.

Tim handed him a copy of the running order.

"I think you'll agree that we *are* treating the matter seriously. Remember we were doing a profile of him."

Somewhat mollified H-P studied the running order, noting with satisfaction his own substantial part in the programme.

"A good decision to let me handle Old Benno on the moral issue. I see that as the core of the whole unhappy aff - er, incident." He got up to leave. "Let me know when Hilda returns."

"I fancy," said Muriel, "that the whole building will know when Hilda returns."

Quentin was next, alert, elegant. He sat on the edge of Tim's desk and lit a Balkan Sobranie. Tim studied his Leslie and Roberts charcoal grey suit, Turnbull and Asser striped shirt and crimson Charvet tie with interest.

"Dressed for the occasion?"

"No, dear heart, merely going out to dinner. Unlike the social riff-raff around here I do not dine in a worn-out boiler suit. The Sixties may be swinging but there's no need for it to be positively threadbare."

"Quite," said Muriel who was the only woman on the programme who didn't wear jeans.

"What's your news?" said Tim.

"Just had a call from Kim, he's totally flummoxed, poor sweet.   Have we all been hoaxed?"

"Could be," said Tim. "All I know is that we are doing a crash programme on the Home Sec."

"And I, dear boy, am I featuring in this exciting exposé?"

"I suppose you couldn't get Kim, could you?"

"Hardly. Would you expect him to prattle on about lovely Wanda and our beloved chairman for instance?"

"What about the chairman?" said Tim.

Quentin looked out of the window.

"Just rumours. I imagine that Wanda has dropped enough on his plate." Deftly changing the subject. "What *can* I do?"

Tim consulted the running order.

"I'd like you to interview some bright young historian about past political sex scandals. Pippa will brief you."

"Don't exactly need too much briefing. Know all about Lulu Harcourt, jolly old Casement and…"

"No, Quentin," said Tim firmly, "just for once can we leave out the boys and go for the girls, as it were, chaps like Parnell and Dilke, who had to resign over women."

"How about Edward VII and Mrs Keppel?"

"Not scandalous," said Tim.

"And Edward VIII and Mrs Simpson?"

"Too scandalous."

"How about a few foreigners?"

"They wouldn't resign even if they were caught doing it in the street and frightening the horses," said Tim.

He put his feet on the desk.

"I think I need a few moments of peace."

It was not to be. Two sedate knocks on the door preceded the entrance of Hopkins, dark suited, suspicious.

"May I come in?"

"You already are in, Hopkins," said Tim wearily. "Have a seat."

Ignoring Muriel, Hopkins glanced disapprovingly round the scruffy office.

"It could do with a lick of paint, I suppose."

"I've heard that before," said Tim.

"It all costs money," said Hopkins alarmed by his rash benevolence. "We're not the BBC, you know."

"I've heard that before," said Tim.

He casually pointed his popgun.

"I imagine I ought to say, 'To what do I owe the pleasure?'"

Hopkins chose to ignore the mild sarcasm.

"We, that is the management, are very concerned about to-night's programme. As you are no doubt fully aware it looks likely to include a mention of the chairman's daughter."

"Nicely put."

"But nevertheless we, that is the management, feel that it would be in everyone's interest to play down as far as possible the, er, role of Lady Alice in what is in effect after all mainly a matter for the government. Do you follow me?"

"Only too well," said Tim.

"Unfortunately," continued Hopkins, "Hilda has not yet returned but the management assume that you will consult closely with her about the content and tone of the programme."

He brushed an imaginary speck of dust from his neatly creased trousers and looked expectantly at Tim.

Tim held the pause.

"Roger."

He fired the popgun. Hopkins, confused, queried, "Roger?"

"It means," said Tim patiently, "according to films I've seen about the RAF, that your message is understood."

Hopkins, suspicious as ever of jokes, nodded briefly and got up to go when the door opened and Ginger put his head round, glimpsed his old enemy and attempted to withdraw.

"Ah, Ruddle, just the man."

Ginger reluctantly entered.

"About your expenses for the Thomas documentary."

"Yes, well…"

"How on earth can you justify spending nearly fifty pounds on a so-called recce of a Member of Parliament?"

"I had to talk to lots of people... all over London," said Ginger defensively.

"Only one bill to show for it, if I remember correctly."

"Yes, said Ginger on safer ground. "Supper for another Welsh M.P., a close friend."

Hopkins adjusted his rimless glasses.

"Even I am aware that that particular M.P. is a distinguished fellow Methodist, an unlikely consumer of four bottles of wine."

"Did I claim that?" said Ginger. "Simple mistake really. Sally must have misread my handwriting." He avoided a glare from Muriel.

"And this enormous taxi bill," continued Hopkins.

"Now that was a genuine mistake. The driver misunderstood my directions and waited outside the restaurant."

"From what I've heard Nick's Bistro is hardly the ideal place to take a Member of Parliament."

"No, as I was trying to explain, that was another meal with a Lobby correspondent," said Ginger feebly.

Hopkins got up to go.

"May I suggest, Ruddle, that you re-do your expenses so that at least Sally can read them and I can believe them."

"Shit," said Ginger as the door closed.

"Serve you right," said Muriel, "and let's have less of blaming Sally."

"Jesus…" began Ginger.

"Bugger off," said Tim, yawning.

In Toby's office Melanie answered the phone and said, "For you, Pippa." The now familiar silky voice of Yvonne said, "Do you think you could pop up and see the chairman?"

Farrier, clearly not at ease, was walking about when she entered the drawing room. He embraced her, offered a drink and sitting beside her on the sofa said, "Sorry, darling, to drag you away from the programme but as you imagine this has come as something of a surprise. I've known of course about Alice… Wanda, but had no idea about old George. Last person in fact I would have thought of … most of the Cabinet are up to something but hardly old George. Who was it who once said that politicians are people who tell lies when they don't have to. Almost sounds like that. Very odd. Anyway there's no chance of a cover-up. At the moment Yvonne is fending off Fleet Street and my wife has gone to the country. Fortunately, as we know, Alice is abroad somewhere."

He took a sip of brandy and soda.

"I'm not suggesting for a moment that the programme should pull any punches. Hilda appears to be away for the day but I've sent a message to Tim Jago. No, what I hoped you could tell me is whether there is a security angle."

Pippa had listened intently. It was clearly not in her interest to disclose any complicity in the matter.

"As far as I know, Archie, there's very little to go on. I believe an opposition M.P. is going to ask the P.M. about rumours but Worthington has already denied that as far as he knew Wanda ever had any foreign connection. She is out of touch and it's very unlikely that any of the Military Attachés will be keen to talk. Least of all surely, Kim Adrian. We're treating it as a straight sex scandal." She grinned. "If you can call any sex scandal straight."

Returning her smile a trifle absently Farrier said, "The only snag now is the security services. Did they know and if they did why didn't they warn George? If they didn't know they're going to look a bit stupid. I somehow think that the P.M. will want to play down the security angle."

He took another drink and smiled, this time fondly. "Thanks, darling. Can I see you this evening?"

"Of course."

"Something pretty special perhaps?"

"Surely."

He watched her slim, long-legged figure saunter across the room, pause in the doorway to wave, and returned pensively to his drink.

Chapter Ten

The news of the resignation was received at MI5 with mixed feelings. The Deputy Director, Watson, badly discredited over the phone-tapping, attended the hurriedly called meeting looking a trifle smug. The junior member who had staked all on a self-promoting leak to MI6 sat silent and anxious.

The Director looked over his half-moon glasses at the committee. "In the first place I think we can congratulate ourselves on some first class investigation which revealed, however regrettably, a possible breach of security by our own Secretary of State. That is now a matter of fact. And yet as you will recall we decided for excellent reasons to, er, consider the matter before proceeding further. I graded the material Most Secret. And yet," he paused surveying the committee, "there has clearly been a leak."

All the members assumed expressions of shifty innocence except the junior member who attempted nonchalance.

"Surely," said the Deputy Director, his self-confidence restored, "this is a case where the end has inadvertently justified the means."

The Director regarded him with distaste.

"I do not consider, Watson, that was the end we had in mind be it never so inadvertent."

The last few words sounded like the translation from a foreign language; the Director hurried on. "I have to tell you that the Prime Minister has requested a report on the matter."

"Do you mean," persisted Watson, "about how we discovered the facts or about how the facts were leaked, be it ever so inadvertently, to the Prime Minister?"

"Surely one cannot leak information *to* a Prime Minister," said a puzzled member. "I thought it worked the other way."

"Please be sensible, gentlemen," said the Director, easily confused. "I am less concerned with the facts than with the leak, isn't that understood?"

"Perhaps," said the junior member, risking the truth, a last resort in the secret world, "MI6 did it." There was a ripple of surprised interest. "How?" someone asked.

"Foreign contacts," said the junior member. "Didn't the Wanda woman have friendships with military attachés?"

"Why would Six want to do that?" asked someone new to the department.

For the first time the Director looked slightly relieved. "A very creditable suggestion. As we all know," he glared at the new member, "Six has always been envious of our competence, particularly in view of their own spectacular failures. I need hardly remind you of Maclean and Burgess."

There was a murmur of approval.

"But…" began Watson.

"What is it, now?" said the Director, irked.

"How do we tell the Prime Minister about a leak of information that we agreed didn't exist in the first place?"

It was what had once been known in military parlance as a 'swift one'. The Director chose to ignore Watson's interruption, mainly because he had no idea how to answer it. Instead he addressed the committee in the voice of authority. "Quite simply I intend to advise the Prime Minister that the information supposedly leaked about the Home Secretary was not considered by us sufficiently damaging for him to take action about himself and therefore the leak should not be regarded as a leak per se since the material had been deemed not to be actionable. Is that clear?"

"Elementary, my dear Watson," murmured the junior member with genuine relief.

Over at MI6 Sir Roderick sent for Carruthers. "First of all you give me this highly damaging information about the Home Secretary. I quite rightly consult the Prime Minister. Then you tell me that the whole thing was a ridiculous publicity stunt by some television company. Now we have the resignation of the Home Secretary. May I ask exactly what is going on?" It was not like this in the Bond novels.

Carruthers fingered his tie. "Our sources were unreliable, I'm afraid, sir."

"You said that it came from what you called our man in MI5, whatever that means."

"It did."

"Surely our job is to evaluate information."

"It is."

Sir Roderick felt that he made a good point. Lacking any training in his job as Head of the Secret Intelligence Service he found it useful to pick up tips from Bond's boss 'M'. This resolute old Admiral was always warning Bond about disinformation.

"Didn't you consider that Five might have done this on purpose?"

"Why would they do that?" asked Carruthers.

"Professional jealousy, my dear fellow. See it everywhere. Out East we always made a point of believing the exact opposite of what the Chinese told us."

"Did that work?"

"Hardly ever. But it confused them and your average Chink doesn't like to be confused."

"I see," said Carruthers.

"So," said Sir Roderick, "I bet your contact was playing that game."

"Possibly," said Carruthers suddenly recalling the deceptive amateurishness of the junior member, the dubious safe house, the interruptions, the "Clarence Rules" nonsense ... why hadn't he suspected something?

"Well, fortunately for you I didn't have the opportunity to tell the PM about your ridiculous mistake. Quite clear after all that poor old George... the er, Home Secretary, made a floater and had to go. Can't say you come out of it well. But at least our yardarm is clear."

He fancied "M" would have approved of that phrase.

"I'm very sorry, Sir Roderick."

"Enough said. Better make sure of your contacts in future."

He nearly added, "Could be a matter of life and death one day," but it smacked too much of that flashy chap '007'.

Carruthers requested an urgent meeting with his Soviet controller. He had fed him contradictory information and he knew only too well how suspicious the KGB were of any behaviour which hinted at a 'double agent'.

Unfortunately by a misunderstanding in the briefing Carruthers walked into that area of the Heath jealously guarded by the sexual marauders, was involved in an unseemly fracas, arrested and charged with gross indecency. Rather than appear in court he hanged himself in his cell with his Old Wykehamist tie. It was a sad end to a promising career.

Old Benno arrived for the programme in high spirits. A politician in a sex scandal was a ripe target for his latest guise as moral crusader.

"H-P apparently wants a serious debate about that old chestnut, the relationship between public and private morality. Trying to put in a good word for poor old George, I suppose. Can't believe the story myself. Wouldn't be surprised if Kim Adrian isn't behind it all."

He took Pippa to one side. "Give me the lowdown, dear girl, you know all the gossip."

"Thanks a lot, Benno, coming from you. Nothing to it. George obviously fell for Wanda, who wouldn't? and got caught red-handed - a rather apt phrase, surely," she added removing Benno's hand from her thigh.

The programme itself had an edge of immediacy not always apparent on routine evenings. It opened with a five-second teaser of Wanda beside a swimming pool in the South of France taken from a home movie and sold by a good friend for an exorbitant price. Back in the studio H-P, looking suitably stern, gave his explanation of the Home Secretary's resignation. This led into a five minute profile of Worthington with still photographs and news clips, from school days, Cambridge, wartime Army service, into merchant banking, marriage and the political years - all of which only emphasised the continuing rectitude of his life. An ITN live insert from a reporter at Westminster gave current reactions of M.P's but could not, regrettably, regale viewers with their actual comments:

"Fancy old George getting his end in there, never knew he had it in him."

"Lucky fellow, often thought I'd liked to have given her one."

"Couldn't afford it, old boy."

"You're never too old for a bit on the side."

"Some bit. At least it was a woman, thank God."

"Give me that number again, will you?"

In the Lords, always competitive with the Commons when it came to adultery, reactions were more casual. "Archie is hardly in a position to give her a wigging, is he?"

"Dim sort of fellow, must have struck lucky."

"At least his daughter's got a job, mine costs me a fortune."

"What did you say her name was?"

Toby interviewed two M.P's "down the line". One, a backbencher friend, expressed surprise, regret and sympathy in well practised terms and the other, an opposition spokesman, who, whilst appearing to show Christian charity, implied that the affair represented the moral delinquency of the entire Cabinet which nothing less than a General Election could resolve. Back in the studio again Quentin prompted a somewhat nervous young history don to recall past political scandals to a point where he found himself speculating inadvisedly on the private life of Anthony Eden. In the gallery Tim said, "For Christ's sake give "Q" a wind before there's a real clanger."

H-P looking magisterial now raised the question of public and private morality, introducing Old Benno as the moral crusader. Unpredictable as ever Benno decided to take a tolerant line despite his habitual contempt for all politicians.

"Let's face it, private lives don't matter. I might even go so far as to say that private lives are often best ignored. Take a well-known example. Our old friend Lloyd George."

H-P's eyebrows went up.

"A persistent adulterer. Yet if he had been forced out of office instead of being made Prime Minister in 1916 Britain might just possibly have lost the war."

"Just possibly," agreed H-P, his loyalty to Wales struggling with his sense of moral superiority.

"Another example," said Benno," of wayward living. Take Churchill."

H-P showed signs of anxiety.

"If Winston had taken to women the way he took to drink in the 1930s he would very probably have been involved in scandal and not been fit for office in 1940. Drink better than sex? Something wrong, surely?"

"Just possibly," said H-P a trifle confused. "But those were exceptional cases. Don't you agree that there must be moral standards which public figures must not only observe but must be seen to observe? Surely they must set an example?"

"Not by moralising. Hubris, my dear H-P. Whenever some public figure preaches a sermon it is inevitably followed by a disaster of some sort. I shouldn't be surprised if someone doesn't one day call for a return to Victorian values. What were *they*? Child brothels, financial greed, moral hypocrisy. Disraeli with his mistresses, Gladstone rescuing prostitutes, the Prince of Wales…"

"Quite so," interrupted H-P hurriedly.

In the gallery Tim said reluctantly, "Better wind this up." In the studio H-P allowed himself some belated words of censure for the Home Secretary.

In the lift afterwards Ziggy said, "Always nice to see you, Mr Benson."

"How are things, Ziggy, my dear fellow?"

"Can't complain. French letters going a bit slow these days. Partly your fault, Mr Benson, you know, with all your religious stuff."

"You'll get your reward in Heaven, Ziggy."

"I do hope so, sir, I really do."

Hilda was already in hospitality making up for lost time. "Damned so-called conference in Tunbridge Wells. I told them a thing or two about blithering amateurs poking their noses into cleaning up television. And what do I come back to?" She glared at Tim, Toby and Pippa who were hastily pouring themselves drinks. "A truly appalling programme. How we ever came to consider doing a profile of this evil man I cannot comprehend. Where is Leo? It was his idea, wasn't it? And as for starting the programme with a disgraceful clip of the chairman's daughter, poor girl ... I don't know how I can bring myself to explain it to Lord Farrier."

"Well..." began Tim, now fortified with a large whisky.

"Be quiet. As I understand only too well from the evening paper which I read in the train the Home Secretary, of all people, after seducing young Alice thinks that by merely resigning he can somehow clear his name. It's monstrous, the man should be hounded out of Parliament if not the country."

Old Benno entered the room with H-P.

"My dear Hilda…"

"Don't you dare dear Hilda me, either of you, after having the nerve to discuss *that man* as though there were the slightest grounds for defending his conduct. I'm surprised at you particularly, Benno, as an upholder of morals -"

"The Home Secretary…" began Benno.

"You know perfectly well that I'm not talking about him," said Hilda furiously. "You tried to forgive Worthington for his appalling behaviour by trying to excuse the real wickedness of Lloyd George"

"Devil's advocate, Hilda," protested Benno.

"Devil's the right word."

She accepted a large gin and tonic from Pippa. "Thank you, my dear, I trust you were not too embarrassed by this unseemliness. I leave the building for a single day and look what happens."

"Be reasonable, Hilda," said Benno in his most deceptively charming tone. "Tim had no option other than to do a programme on a very serious subject and - let me finish - he did it extremely well. After all we came out on balance against the wretched man. You yourself said only the other day," he added piously, "that we should never forget compassion in our programmes as well as our daily lives."

Hilda looked momentarily puzzled. "When did I say that? Well, perhaps I did have to remind the Archbishop before he appeared on Forum the other evening that even homosexuals are human beings."

At that moment Quentin entered with the young historian and Hilda weaved menacingly towards him. "Are you aware young man, whoever you are, that you have very probably landed us with a considerable libel action apart from a gratuitous," the word came out slightly slurred, "insult to one of Britain's finest Prime Ministers, whom I'm still happy to call a friend."

"He only..." began Quentin.

"Be quiet. And *you* should have not let him start talking nonsense about living politicians. The dead were bad enough."

"Hilda," said Quentin firmly, "he only mentioned Eden's divorce to illustrate the changing attitude to social stigmas."

"Lord Avon to you," said Hilda, not to be outdone. "I dislike inaccuracies. Yes, what is it Yvonne?"

The elegant secretary hovered at her side. "Mrs Fenn, the chairman wonders if you could spare a moment."

"Of course, of course," said Hilda collecting herself. "I expect," she added sharply to Tim, "a full report and transcript first thing tomorrow."

She sailed unsteadily out of the room and it was as if the "All Clear" had sounded after a heavy wartime raid. Conversation broke out on all sides and glasses were urgently refilled. Some while later amongst the emptying bottles Simon and Sally prepared to leave.

"Come and have some supper, Pip," said Sally.

"Sorry, got a sort of date."

"Hope it's sort of fun," said Simon.

"You might say that," said Pippa.

Later Yvonne said, "Go in, darling, he's expecting you."

Lord Farrier was smiling reflectively as he opened the champagne. "Dear Hilda, she really is a hoot. Endless apologies about the programme, particularly that rather good clip of Alice at the beginning. Loads of sympathy for me having a daughter debauched by a Cabinet minister. Barely keep a straight face. Main problem is to steer her away from the press. I've spoken to the P.M., he was sorry to hear about Alice and doesn't think there's anything in the security thing. Bit of nonsense of old Roddy's, new in the job and all that. Anyway, darling, enough shop. Here's to you.

They touched glasses and sat down on the sofa. "Have you thought of anything special?"

"Been a bit busy, I'm afraid," said Pippa.

"No matter. I'd rather like an old favourite."

"How old?"

"Five thousand years, I believe," said Farrier smiling.

"Not possible."

"It's called the Chinese Circle of Joy."

"Vaguely heard of it. Can't say I've tried."

"Quite fun," said Farrier refilling their glasses. "Needs three or more of course. That's why Yvonne has stayed. Do you find her attractive?"

"I do, come to think of it," said Pippa.

Farrier pressed a bell on his desk and minutes later Yvonne entered wearing a cheong-sam, the slit skirt displaying her long slender legs. "More a triangle this evening, I suppose. Do you remember, Archie, when we once had ten, quite a Who's Who of politicos, film stars and that Duke and his ghastly wife - before their pretty juicy divorce?"

"The headless man?" asked Pippa.

"Not me," said Farrier. "The betting at White's was on Duncan but I forget who won. Let's go into the bedroom."

It was spacious, silky, mirrored softly-lit Second Empire style with a luxuriously large bed. A blow-up of Bosch's Garden of Delights and erotica by Courbet and Boucher decorated the walls. On her first visit Pippa had made the obvious comparison with a high-class brothel.

"Exactly," said Farrier, pleased. "Many years ago my father took me to Paris and a brothel used exclusively, I think, by the Jockey Club. I had my first woman in a room rather like this and I thought that one day I'll have a copy," he looked round gratified,"and I did."

Finale

Next morning Simon and Sally went into Metro together; she had stayed the night. "Darling, you really must do something about this dreadful attic of yours."

"Not worth the bother."

"What about the landlord?"

"Tough old Yorkshire man," said Simon, "not one for spending his brass. I met him in the hall recently looking at the tatty Victorian wallpaper and when I asked him if he was going to replace it he said he couldn't because he had been told it was genuine Colin Morris."

"Well, you'd better move in with me."

"Do you mean that?"

"I wouldn't have bloody well offered would I if I didn't mean it?"

Simon kissed her. "Will you marry me?"

"No. Anyway not just yet. We'd better see what the hell's going on at Metro."

Wendy was on duty in the lobby. "Have you got a ciggy, my nerves are terrible. It's really Kitty's day on but she's got the curse or something," adding, "lucky girl."

The telephone began ringing.

"Oh, God."

They passed Ziggy at the lift gates. "Bit of a night, eh? I thought Mr Jago would never make it to the taxi. How about a Ronson with spare flints, only three quid?"

Even Fred the boilerman had heard of the night's events. "It's working in television that does it, I told you. And old Mrs Fenn, bless her, got stuck in the bin room next to the toilets by mistake."

They found Muriel packing up in Tim's office. "What's this?"

"Tim's going to edit Forum and Andrew's taking over."

"Rotten luck."

"Not really," said Muriel packing the popgun and backscratcher, "He needs a rest. Might even ease up on the drink."

"And Leo?"

"Gone to Granada. Been angling for a job there."

Toby was scanning the morning papers. Headlines ranged from *Home Secretary in Sex Scandal, Unworthy Worthington Disgrace, Whither Wanda?*" to *Resignation of Senior Minister* in "*The Times*. Lawyers had carefully vetted copy about Wanda. After all, no one had yet managed to speak to her, there was no actual proof of her being a call-girl (merely police tip-offs) and she had a powerful millionaire father with easy access to sharp Q.C.s

One newspaper with better paid informers than most got wind of the MI5 angle and ran an inside page story under *Home Sec. Phone Tap Shock*.

In the editor's office of the great newspaper the lines were humming from Arizona. Why hadn't he known? What did he know? Where was Wanda? Who was on the story? How had Farrier got away with it? Why, what, when, how...? the rasping voice ate up the thousands of miles between Tucson and London.

The editor became a demon. Finally a high-price stringer in the Caribbean by dint of hiring a flying-boat, chartering a yacht and bribing every French official in sight, got a telephone call through to Nikki's private island near Martinique. It was not a convenient moment for either of them in the poolside shower when a servant announced the call. Nikki was about to tell him to ring off when Wanda stood up saying, "They'll only go on ringing, darling." She slipped on a wrap and reached for the nearby phone.

Yes, it was perfectly true she had known George Worthington as a friend for many years, she was sorry to hear he had resigned but failed to understand the connection, perhaps there had been a misunderstanding, she could not recall meeting military attachés unless it had been at one of her father's receptions. No, she did not know when she would be back. Marriage to Nikki? Not on the cards at the moment. Thanks for ringing. She rejoined Nikki in the shower.

Frustrated on the Wanda story the papers picked up the scent on the Kim Adrian trail until it was discovered that Kim had recently provided a night club hostess for the chairman of one of the newspapers and that line of enquiry was killed instantly in all the papers.

The obvious target was poor old George secluded on his Somerset estate where loyal farm hands kept reporters at bay, on one occasion firing a twelve-bore over the head of a photographer perched on a hayrick. Archives were ransacked for pictures and a so-called friend sold for a hefty price a wartime snapshot of George beside the swimming pool at the Gezira Sporting Club in Cairo with a bathing beauty friendly to King Farouk. He did not bother to explain that she had merely stopped to pass a message to his commanding officer, a colonel of legendary depravity.

Mostly the papers printed their gossip column pictures of Wanda. *Society Model in Political Scandal* was about a near as they could get to the facts. Lord Farrier when finally contacted on the steps of White's expressed regret at the downfall of a friend, tinged with surprise and sadness (shared of course by his wife) that their much loved daughter should have been involved. He agreed readily with the editorials that were deploring the falling standards in both public and private life. He liked to think that his own television company made every effort to uphold those standards. Yes, he intended to speak on moral issues in the Lords quite soon. And now if they'd excuse him he had an urgent appointment. He sank back in the waiting car. "South Kensington."

That afternoon in the Commons the Prime Minister made a dignified and sympathetic statement about the long and admirable service rendered by George Worthington to country and party, a career abruptly cut short by an act of human frailty. An opposition member tried to raise the matter of security but was conveniently ruled out of order by the Speaker on procedural grounds which few journalists could follow. The House returned to the debate on dog licences.

Later that evening the Prime Minister and the director of MI6 met up again in Pratt's. "If I may say so, Eddie, I thought you made a first-class show in the House."

"Thanks, Roddy, glad to hear it. Seemed to go down quite well. Tricky, these moral things, I reckon." They paused over the port.

"Think I owe you an apology, Eddie."

"Why's that?" said the Prime Minister.

"Well, looking back on the matter I rather wish I'd played my cards a bit differently."

"In what way?"

"Touch of discretion. After all, old George wasn't exactly doing any harm ... a little fling with a giddy young girl hardly likely to involve state secrets. Inexperience on my part in the job, I fear."

"My dear Roddy, you mustn't reproach yourself. You did what you thought fit. MI6 is about that sort of thing, isn't it? Spies and so on. Can't say that I go along with it. Do you remember before the war one of Roosevelt's Secretaries of State, can't recall his name, was asked about code-breaking and he replied that gentlemen don't read each other's mail. Thought it rather amusing at the time. I feel the same now about all this spying. Willie Maugham told me that it was the most monotonous work he'd ever done. I suppose we must have spies because everyone else does but, you know, the only justification seems to be that they check out whether the other chap is bluffing, if you follow me."

"Quite so," said Roddy, not following him at all. There was another pause broken by a member saying, "Thought you were in China or somewhere, Roddy."

"No, I'm here."

"Good to see you back."

"Thanks."

Roddy studied his glass.

"That's really what I wanted to talk to you about, Eddie."

"China?"

"In a way. I've been thinking perhaps this job isn't really my cup of tea. Not a desk wallah, you might say. Better off in the field."

The Prime Minister refilled his glass.

"Sorry to hear you say that. I quite understand the feeling. Often have it myself in Cabinet, I wonder what on earth I'm doing sitting indoors when I could be out on the moors. Where were you thinking of?"

"Ulan Bator, as a matter of fact."

"Your old stamping ground."

"Exactly."

The Prime Minister gave Roddy a benevolent glance.

"I meant to ask you, do you get any shooting out there?"

"Ptarmigan mostly."

"Not quite the same."

"Not quite."

In the Citadel a hundred dark-suited figures were gloomily shifting the usual load of paperwork across their polished pine desks. Phones rang, telexes clattered and plain, stout women carried glasses of lemon tea to favoured individuals one of whom was now studying a 'flash' message.

"Urgent from Source One, Ivan."

"All traffic from the London Embassy seems to be urgent. Bad news, I suppose, Dimitri."

"Very bad. At least I think so. It is not easy to decide how much is disinformation."

"I thought it was up to us to handle the disinformation."

"Yes, Ivan, but how can we do that if we don't know what information is correct in the first place?"

"Is not material from Source One always correct?"

"Yes, except when it is meant to be used as disinformation."

"What is it this time, Dimitri?"

"It says that all previous material from Bulldog must be discounted."

"Why?"

"Apparently Bulldog's contact was using disinformation - but only accidentally."

"How was that?"

"Bulldog's contact's contact was misled by his own most secret information."

"So, in fact, the most secret information was in all probability itself disinformation."

"Very probably, Ivan."

They both sipped their lemon teas reflectively. "What did we do with previous Bulldog material, Dimitri?"

"We filed it in the Gulag cabinets."

"So we did. That was a clever move."

"A very clever move, Ivan."

"No one will ever know."

"Except you and me."

"And Bulldog?"

Dimitri chuckled. "We will see that he goes to the real Gulag."

The man who was reading the latest Ian Fleming novel said, "Their agent Bond has killed our best spy."

"Do not worry, Leon Leonovitch, I have it on good authority that Bond is a mole."

"He seems to spend a lot of time with beautiful women," said Leon wistfully.

"That is a bluff too. As I told you he was at their Eton school."

Simon's last day at Metro was one of those autumn mornings which almost reconcile the grumbling public to English weather: pale blue sky, a low dazzling sun and cool, crisp air. Wendy was on duty again, unusually cheerful among the ringing telephones and importunate visitors. Her good news, intimate and reassuring, had occurred that morning; she longed to tell someone but Simon wasn't a suitable confidant.

"You couldn't be a sweetie and get me a cheese sandwich or something from the canteen. Kitty's still away and I haven't had a bite to eat and now everyone's changing their extensions and I don't know what-all."

"You can leave me off the list."

"Darling, have you been sacked?"

"Not yet. I merely thought it was time to go."

"I am sorry," said Wendy grappling a telephone. "Don't forget the cheese sandwich."

Ziggy saluted.

"Sorry to hear you're off, sir. Bit of a short stay but they do come and go here. I reckon I'm quite a veteran apart of course from Mrs Fenn." He chuckled. "Why, I can remember her when I started here, she was a producer on gardening programmes."

"A bit milder in those days, I imagine."

"Lord love us, no. She once threw a flower pot across the studio at the floor manager."

"Was he hurt?" asked Simon.

"Not so hurt as funny in the head. He retired soon afterwards."

Simon found Pippa and Ginger in the canteen. "Cheer up," Pippa was saying. "You had a good recce."

"Christ!" exploded Ginger. "Hopkins won't even pass my expenses. I've a good mind to bloody resign."

"Darling, don't be silly. If you remember the last time you did they very nearly accepted it. Come back to Good Evening, you like Andrew don't you?"

"Not as much as Tim. He's not a drinker, is he?"

"Can't have everything," said Pippa. "Simon, dear, get us some more coffee, will you?"

"And why don't *you* stay on," she asked when he returned. "Andrew wants you to, he told me."

"I don't know. Feel like a change," said Simon in no particular tone of voice.

"Not back to advertising, surely?"

"Jesus, no. Thought I might have a crack at the BBC, there's a job going at Lime Grove, I hear."

"Better you than me," said Ginger, "the corporation is stuffed with people like Hopkins."

"I don't know," said Pippa, "they're doing this late-night show at week-ends, looks fun."

"They've also got their own version of Hilda," said Ginger not to be outdone.

"Not possible?" queried Simon.

"They say she once chucked a guest out of hospitality by the scruff of the neck."

"Why?"

"He praised an ITV programme."

"Hey," said Ginger without looking at his watch," I reckon the bar's open."

The club was filling up with the usual Friday drinking crowd. Hilda was holding forth to H-P, Toby and Quentin. "Excellent choice by the Prime Minister. I've known Giles Morton since he entered the House. Honourable, diligent, happily married. I don't really understand why the P.M. didn't give him the Home Office in the first place," she glared round, possibly looking for Leo, "instead of that monster. Giles is a true gentleman."

"Indeed," said H-P. "Like ... Lord Farrier."

"Exactly," said Hilda. "And it's a feather in our cap that he's agreed to Penetration. I trust they will make the most of it, H-P."

"Indeed."

Quentin caught Toby's eye.

"They did a very clever sketch about old George Worthington on that BBC late-night show."

"Trust you to be watching that rubbish, Quentin," said Hilda, unusually indulgent. I'm told, I've never of course watched it, that they show no respect for politicians. As I've said before, I don't know how Hugh allows it."

"He's a clever chap," said Quentin.

"Hugh?"

"No, Hilda, the chap who invented this late-night thing."

"Too clever by half, if you ask me," said Hilda. "I imagine he's rather like you, trying to mix politics and light entertainment."

"I take that as a compliment, Hilda," said Quentin offering to refill her glass.

"Well, it wasn't intended. Thank you, Quentin." She watched him go to the bar. "You know he tried an idea like that on me some months ago. I said to him at the time, and I'm afraid the BBC will soon realise it, that once you lose respect for politicians, the good ones of course, you strike at the heart of democracy. I'm told, and it's hardly credible, that one of their actors did a barely concealed take-off of the Prime Minister."

"Very funny," said Toby.

"That's quite enough from you, young man," said Hilda accepting her drink from Quentin. "There are times when you go too far."

At that moment Ginger caught her eye.

"Come here."

Ginger approached her cautiously.

"Have you finished that little documentary on, who was it, the M.P.?

"Well…"

"Don't interrupt. I've got something more urgent for you to do. The other evening at a party I met a nice young actor Richard something, I didn't catch his name. Charming man, high spirited, talked a lot about Wales for some reason, and came up with the suggestion that we do a programme about Dylan Thomas. Of course I put forward my objections as you well know but he was very convincing. Apparently the poet was only what he called a social drinker. Anyway this young actor offered to do the commentary, he had quite a nice voice." Ginger had managed to repress a smile. "So, despite my previous misgivings I am allowing you to do this. A serious documentary, mind you, not just a collection of doubtful anecdotes. You might do worse than begin by meeting this young actor perhaps over a drink, and I mean *a* drink." Hilda looked pointedly at Ginger's pint glass. "And make sure the fee for the commentary is the usual one, five guineas at most, I think."

"Yes, Hilda."

"Well, that's settled. Quite fortunate for the young actor meeting me like that, it should help his career. He said something about films but as I told him it's a chancy business particularly in America."

Simon and Sally were having a farewell drink at the bar with Tim and Pippa.

"It all started with booze, I seem to remember," said Tim, "so it might as well finish that way."

"I'm very grateful," said Simon.

"What for?"

"My intro to telly."

"What did you make of it?"

"Well…" began Simon, but his views were not to be known.

"Gossiping," barked a familiar voice. Hilda had approached unobserved.

"Actually we were discussing television," said Tim.

"Ah, the face of the future as I was telling the conference the other day..." but even Hilda's views were mercifully not to be known for she had caught sight of the clock. "Is that really the time. I'm lunching with H-P. Which reminds me," she eyed Simon. "The catering standards are slipping again. I expected better things of you." She left.

"Dear Simon," said Tim. "First the New York Office and then catering manager ... what next?"

"How about another round," said Ginger emptying his glass.